SAVING DANI

The One I Want

ELLIE MASTERS

JEM Publishing

We believe in Soulmates, True Love & Romance.

Editor: Erin Toland

Interior Design/Formatting: Ellie Masters

Published in the United States of America

JEM Publishing

ISBN: 978-1-952625-33-6

 Created with Vellum

Dedication

This book is dedicated to my one and only—my amazing and wonderful husband.

Thank you, my dearest love, my heart and soul, for putting up with me, for believing in me, and for loving me.

You pushed me when I needed to be pushed. You supported me when I felt discouraged. You believed in me when I didn't believe in myself.

If it weren't for you, this book never would have come to life.

Books by Ellie Masters

The LIGHTER SIDE

Ellie Masters is the lighter side of the Jet & Ellie Masters writing duo! You will find Contemporary Romance, Military Romance, Romantic Suspense, Billionaire Romance, and Rock Star Romance in Ellie's Works.

YOU CAN FIND ELLIE'S BOOKS HERE:

ELLIEMASTERS.COM/BOOKS

Military Romance

Guardian Hostage Rescue Specialists

Rescuing Melissa

(Get a FREE copy of Rescuing Melissa

when you join Ellie's Newsletter

https://elliemasters.com/RescuingMelissa)

Rescuing Zoe

Rescuing Moira

Rescuing Eve

Rescuing Lily

Rescuing Jinx

Rescuing Maria

Military Romance

Guardian Personal Protection Specialists

Sybil's Protector

The One I Want Series

(Small Town, Military Heroes)

By Jet & Ellie Masters

Rockstar Romance

The Angel Fire Rock Romance Series

Contemporary Romance

Billionaire Romance

Billionaire Boys Club

Richard

Brody

Contemporary Romance

Cocky Captain

(Vi Keeland & Penelope Ward's Cocky Hero World)

Romantic Suspense

EACH BOOK IS A STANDALONE NOVEL.

The Starling

~AND~

Science Fiction

Ellie Masters writing as L.A. Warren

Vendel Rising: a Science Fiction Serialized Novel

ONE

Dax

FLORIDA'S EVER-PRESENT HUMIDITY AND OPPRESSIVE HEAT CLOTS THE air and makes the scars on my back itch. I swipe at my brow, flicking sweat off the tips of my fingers, and glare at the Military Personnel building.

This is my last official military act, an ignominious end to a career full of sacrifice, heroism, and selfless service to my country.

A female officer approaches and I snap a pristine salute to the unknown second lieutenant.

"Ma'am." My Texas twang vibrates in the air, bringing an attention grabbing smile from the woman.

The pretty lieutenant is years younger than me and returns my salute with much less alacrity than the crispness of mine. Her eyes widen at the scar on my face, a jolt of horror, but then her gaze slips to my toned physique and a sly smile slips out. My face might be trashed, but women still like a well-built man.

With the exception of her wince at the scar, I'm used to that kind of reaction from women. I know exactly what she sees and how the gears in her head churn wondering if the stories are true about the stamina of men such as me.

They are.

Not that she'll find out.

The entirety of my life has been dedicated to being in the best physical condition possible. I have what others call an imposing presence and my buddies claim women find me easy on the eye. I don't know about that last part, but the first is true. I turn heads everywhere I go. I better. Other people's lives depend on it.

Or, they did.

I barely register the impact of what the lieutenant's gaze means. I'm not interested in chasing some nameless lieutenant into bed. Although, from the look the baby officer gives me, a romp in the sheets is mine for the taking.

They're all like that.

Women who see the maroon beret, and make the connection with what it implies, want the bragging rights which come from saying they slept with a man in special ops.

I have other concerns on my mind. Like what the hell I'm going to do with the rest of my life.

The pretty officer stops, her mouth opening to lure me in, but I keep my attention focused straight ahead, intent on my purpose, and march away, leaving her to wipe the drool from her chin.

For me, this is the end. There will be no celebration, either with alcohol flowing in my veins or a woman filling my bed.

The rim of the maroon beret dampens with my sweat and my Air Force uniform clings to my skin. A badge of honor, the beret designates me as one of the most elite in the special forces community.

I won't wear the beret after today, or my uniform.

After everything I gave to my country, the United States Air Force decided too much damage makes me unworthy of continued service. Some of those injuries are forever etched in the scars decorating my back. Other, more concerning, damage hides in the cracks of my mind.

During my exit physical, my doctor tried to explain how the trauma locked in my head made me a liability to my team, and damn if I don't agree.

Doesn't mean I didn't fight to stay.

But in the end, I lost against the bureaucracy of a military medical system caught between balancing the needs of the mission against the injuries military service inflicted on its Airmen—on me.

Cool air conditioning blows down on me as I enter the Military Personnel building. A quick check of the directory and I find my way to the waiting room for Military Separations. I sign in and take a seat.

One hour later, I exit with honorable discharge papers in hand and an uncertain future staring me in the face.

My cell phone rings. One glance at the screen and my lips draw back. I don't need a lecture from my old man.

Not now.

Not ever.

Not that my father cares what I think about anything.

"Dax." I answer with my nickname, more of a reflex than anything else and cringe. My father will surely have something to say about that.

"Alexander." My father's deep voice rumbles across thousands of miles, heavy with a lifetime's worth of judgment threaded in four simple syllables.

One word.

My name.

A name I hate.

Alexander.

That's all it takes to send me back to the vulnerable ten-year-old who wanted nothing more than to hear my father say my name with pride. Seth Kingston never did, and I learned long ago I'll never earn my father's love.

A child shouldn't have to work so hard for a father's approval. The man I am now most certainly doesn't care to start.

"Father." Never dad, or daddy. I was always forced to be formal with my father. I keep my response to a single word, not encouraging conversation.

"Your mother says we'll be expecting you." Disappointment hangs heavy in those words.

With the Air Force behind me, I have nowhere to go but home, but my father makes it sound like an unwelcome event.

I called my mother a week ago. She begged me to come home. It's been years since I've been to the ranch, and I have no intention of returning anytime soon. In the end, her tears made me promise to visit.

I won't stay. I can't, but I'll come home for a little while. At least until I figure out what comes next.

"Yes, sir."

"Do you mind telling me when we may expect you?"

A stiff formality hangs between me and my father. The brusqueness of the question irritates me, not that I should expect anything else.

I didn't give my mother a definite date. I can be there in a few hours if I hop on a plane, but I'm in no rush to go home. Not when it means staring into my father's eyes and seeing the proof of everything my father believes etched in the hard, unforgiving lines of his craggy face.

I am not a failure. No matter what my father believes.

I'm a war decorated hero, one of the very few awarded the Air Force Cross, the second highest military award that can be given to a member of the Air Force and I wear it with pride. It's awarded for extraordinary heroism in combat and I earned the honor.

Not that my father cares.

All my father sees is a son who the Air Force kicked out for being unworthy.

I need a moment before heading home.

"I'm driving, so a few days." I don't have a vehicle. I sold my previous car before the last deployment to save on insurance, but I'll buy some piece of crap if only to delay my arrival by a few days.

"Can you be more specific?" My father grinds out the words.

Can you be less of an ass?

"No, sir. I have a few things to tie up here. When I hit the road, I'll give mother a call and let her know when to expect me." Unlike my father, my mother smothers me in love and praises all my achievements. I'd stay home if it weren't for my father.

And if I work things out, I can waste nearly a week before I have to pass beyond the heavy gates of Kingston Ranch, Texas's largest cattle ranching operation. Someday, it'll pass to me. At least, if my father doesn't write me out of the will before then.

"Please do that. You know how she doesn't like surprises."

My mother doesn't care. The best surprise will be to see her son come home unannounced. She lives for shit like that. Unlike my father, she doesn't need advance notice to *prepare* for my homecoming.

What my mother sees in my father I'll never understand. She claims it was love at first sight, something I don't believe in. But to my father's credit, that man puts Elizabeth Kingston on a pedestal. He moves heaven and earth to make sure her life is as perfect as it can be.

For that reason alone, I grant grudging respect for my father, and may even look up to him. Despite the way Seth Kingston treats his one and only son, he's the perfect husband.

"Yes, sir. I will call as soon as I know." It's best to agree with my father and not give any reason to start an argument.

"Good. When you get here, we need to talk."

He doesn't want to talk. There's nothing good my father has to say, but I keep all emotion from my voice and give the easiest answer.

"Yes, sir."

Without a goodbye, my father ends the call, leaving me to consider my next step. Medically discharged, it's time to come to terms with the fact I can no longer do the job I was trained for in the military.

A quick stop at a used car dealership off-base and I drive away from Egland Air Force Base in a beat-up pickup truck with more rust than paint. I hit the road, then veer off when I spy a sign for an SPCA shelter.

My doc wants me to sign up for one of those wounded warrior companion animal programs, but I don't want to be associated with *wounded* anything. It would be admitting I have a problem, but I'm not so arrogant to think a dog might not help ease the loneliness an uncertain future brings.

The woman at the shelter greets me with the same hungry expression as the baby lieutenant. With her eyes sparking with attraction, and her cheeks turning pink, she asks me about dogs.

"What are you looking for?" Her lashes flutter over the arch of her cheeks as she tries not to stare.

"Just a mutt, ma'am." I want a reject like me.

"Well, do you want a large dog, small dog? Something in between?"

"No ankle biters and nothing too big. I like smart dogs with energy."

Her eyes light up. "Oh, we might have the perfect dog for you."

"Take me to her."

"It's a him. Is that a problem?"

"Nope. It doesn't really matter." Bitches are easier to control, but I can make it work. I grew up around cattle dogs my entire life. On a ranch with tens of thousands of cattle, dogs do a lion's share of the work. I'll take what I can get.

"Well, this one is a Blue Heeler."

What are the chances this pound has a herding dog? It feels like fate has a hand in this. Blue Heelers were originally developed in Australia, but are now used extensively in America because of their innate skill in driving cattle over long distances and across rough terrain.

"You don't say?"

"Yes, he's a bit high strung."

Blue Heelers have high energy and incredible endurance for medium-sized dogs. Their short coats help the dogs manage barb wire, brambles, and thorny underbrush easily.

"I can imagine."

"Are you familiar with the breed?"

I grew up with Blue Heelers. It has to be fate.

"As a matter of fact, I am." I'm not one to believe in fate, but this might be a sign.

"Well, he was brought in because he was too energetic for his previous owners. They said he kept running off. Good news is he's already chipped and neutered. Has all his shots too."

"That's cool. And can I adopt today?" I don't want to endure filling out an application asking about where I live. As of an hour ago, I have no home.

"Normally, there's a process." She takes in my Air Force uniform, the beret on my head, and smiles. "But, I'm sure he'll be going to a good home."

"Well, if he has the energy to burn, I'm the man for him." Every day begins with a ten-mile run, and that's simply the warm up for what comes next. "Does the dog have a name?"

"His previous owners didn't leave one. Said they didn't want to influence his new owner, but he's a bundle of energy, a real dynamo, and keeps us busy."

"I like that name."

"What name?"

"Dynamo." It sounds like the perfect name for the kind of dog I need. "Show me the dog."

An hour later, Dynamo jumps into my new beat up half ton pickup truck. He licks my hand and smears nose prints on the window before settling down. I stop at the local pet superstore and load up the pickup with food for Dynamo. I toss a dog bed, leash, and chew toys in the back seat and a rope toy to keep Dynamo busy during the long drive. Dynamo sports a brand new collar, with his name and my cell phone number embroidered on it.

Dynamo sniffs the rope toy, gives it a lick or two, then puts his head in my lap. He stares up at me with soulful eyes until I reach down and scratch behind his ears.

"Guess it's just you and me, now."

I rub Dynamo's neck and pull onto the freeway. The open road calls to me. Depending on how hard I push, we can make it to Texas in a couple of days, but a restlessness churns in my gut.

I'm not ready to go home.

Starting off in Florida, there are only a few directions to go. We could head north, up the eastern coastline, but I'm not ready to deal with that many people. Heading due west would bring us to Texas, and I'm not ready to face the obligations of home.

"Well Dynamo, what do you think?"

Letting the dog decide may not be the best decision, but I give it a go. Each time we reach an intersection, I leave the decision to Dynamo. The only rule is nowhere headed east.

Four days later, we find ourselves driving past Billings, Montana, and breezing through the small town of Peace Springs. Nothing like what we have in Texas, they raise cattle here too. At least I'm familiar with that. I question the pasture sporting llamas munching grass. Who knows what got into these northerner's minds about that?

But even the small town of Peace Springs has too many people for me. People make my skin crawl and the smallest thing seems to trigger the post-traumatic stress I still refuse to fully acknowledge. Dynamo helps in that regard, seeming to develop a keen sense of when my nerves get the better of me. We spend a lot of time cooped up in that beat up pickup truck.

"Bear Creek." I pause at the sign to the small town and look to my dog. "How does that sound?"

Dynamo cocks his head and his ears lift. He gives a soft yip and licks the passenger side window.

"You think that's a good place to stop for the night?"

Dynamo's tail wags.

TWO

Dani

—————

TEARS STREAM DOWN MY CHEEKS. WHAT BEGAN AS A PROPOSAL ended in a betrayal of the worst possible kind. The night of the Spring Formal, Scott McDonnell got down on one knee, ring in hand, love spilling from his filthy lips, and proposed.

—————

"DANI, WILL YOU BE MINE?"

"Yes!"

—————

MY EXCITED SCREAM ECHOED IN MY EARS. I DIDN'T KNOW ABOUT HIS betrayal then.

Scott's first cousin, Beth, came to Washington State Campus to take a look around. A senior in high school, she was interviewing for the incoming Freshman class. Scott invited Beth to stay in his apartment and I thought nothing of it.

Why should I?

The two of them are family, first cousins, and there should be no issue.

Asking Beth to accompany us to the Spring Formal seemed weird, and wasn't my idea, but Scott wanted to give Beth the full college experience. Since I'll soon be a part of Scott's family, it seemed the right thing to do. Besides, I was still riding on the high of Scott's proposal.

We dated on an off during our undergraduate years and through my first three years of veterinarian school in the WIMU program. A combined program between Washington State University, the University of Idaho, Montana State University, and Utah State University, WIMU forms the Regional Program in Veterinary Medicine for the northwestern states. I'm one of only ten students admitted from Montana and can't wait to finish and begin my practice on my father's ranch near Bear Creek.

My first year in the WIMU program Scott and I dealt with the difficulties of a long distance relationship. My second, and now third year, we reunited at WSU. He's finishing up a masters program in business and finance while I continue my classroom and clinical study in the combined WIMU program. My last, and final year will consist of clinical placements throughout the four-state region.

We discussed what that last year of separation might mean for us. Not that it's a problem. The future belonged to us, and while I expected a ring on my finger by graduation, Scott surprised me by giving it to me a year early.

———————

"OUR FAMILIES FIT PERFECTLY TOGETHER, DANI. WITH MY FAMILY'S resources and your father's land, great things are in store for us."

———————

SCOTT'S FAMILY HAS BANKING CONTACTS IN BOZEMAN AND MY father has his ranch. I'm not clear how those two mesh, but Scott seems confident about our future. My father likes Scott too. As an only child, that works perfectly.

Everything was perfect.

I can tend to the veterinary needs of the ranch while Scott uses his mind for business to run the cattle operation.

We're well matched. A perfect pair. Little did I know what my future held as far as Scott went.

I smiled and admired the glittering facets of the two-carat ring propped on my finger. Then Beth walked in, stealing the show in an overly revealing dress with a slit running nearly to her hip.

Beth is one of those natural beauties. Scott always goes on and on about how his cousin is supermodel hot. If Beth wasn't related to him, I would be jealous. They're remarkably close cousins.

I was such a fool.

Beth accompanied us to the Spring Formal and Scott grinned the entire evening with two women draped on his arms. Normally, I would've gone back to his place at the end of the night, but Scott asked me not to spend the night. He didn't think it sent the right message to his impressionable cousin.

Not that Beth is innocent, and not that Beth didn't flirt with every man in attendance. But Scott didn't want Beth sleeping on the couch in his one bedroom apartment. He gave her his bed and took the couch. It made sense at the time. Scott dropped me off at my apartment, then he and Beth returned to his.

That was the Friday before spring midterms. Midterms I probably failed in the aftermath of what happened next.

Waking early the next day, I went straight to the library. All my exams were bunched at the beginning of exam week. It's tough because I have five exams crammed into three days, but it'll be worth it when my Spring Break starts two days before everyone else.

My mistake was leaving one of my books at Scott's apartment. I needed a break and hoped to catch him and Beth for lunch before hitting the books for the rest of the day.

At his apartment, there was no sign of Scott or Beth, and to my surprise, his bed was perfectly made. Scott never makes his bed. But it made sense since he gave Beth the bed and slept on the couch.

For some reason, the skin between my shoulder blades itched. There were no blankets on the couch. No pillow either. I should've left, but a folded note on one of the pillows caught my eye. I shouldn't look, but couldn't stop as I picked up the note and read.

Scott,

I will never forget last night. It was everything and more than I ever thought it would be. It will be our little secret.

Forever and Always yours,

Beth.

There were many ways to interpret that note, but I knew. The sinking feeling in my gut told me the truth. Crumpling the note in my hand, I shoved it deep into my pocket, not sure what I would do, or how I would confront Scott.

The rest of the day was a waste. I obsessed over that note and tried convincing myself the thoughts swirling in my head were wrong.

They're cousins. First cousins. And cousins don't do the things I think they did.

Beth left later that day.

I made an excuse when Scott asked me to dinner. I had to cram for my tests. He wanted to come over Saturday night to study, which means he wants sex. That twisted my stomach.

Thinking about him sleeping with Beth and then crawling into my bed made me retch over the toilet for over an hour. Tears pour from my eyes and snot runs from my nose. My stomach twists and churns. I empty the contents of my stomach until there's nothing left.

I avoid him on Sunday, saying I have study groups with the other vet students. Some of that is true, and those study sessions might be the only thing that save my ass when the test results come back. I won't know until after Spring Break.

Two exams down on Monday.

More excuses not to see Scott see him pushing harder for time alone with his new fiancée.

Fiancée?

With a tug and more tears, I rip the ring off my finger. I managed to make it through my two exams on Tuesday before I could no longer put off the conversation I needed to have.

"I've missed you." Scott pulls me into a hug and my entire body stiffens. "What's wrong? You look exhausted." He dips down, getting eye level with me and gives a slow, lazy blink.

Don't cry. Be strong. Don't cry.

Doubt creeps in. Maybe I read the whole situation wrong?

Maybe he did sleep on the couch? Maybe Scott and Beth's unusual closeness is simply because they grew up together?

That makes it worse.

And I'm exhausted because I barely sleep thinking about him and Beth doing things in bed together, a bed he shares with me. A shiver ripples down my spine.

The crumpled note is still in my bag. I take it out and hand it to him.

"What's this?"

"You tell me."

I give him a flat stare. Heat fills my cheeks. Righteous anger is followed by hot pinpricks behind my lids. I squeeze my eyes tight and fight off my tears.

"I can't believe you did that."

His eyes widen as he scans the note, then he glances at me, a look of horror and guilt splashes across his cheating face.

"It's not what it looks like."

"It's disgusting."

THE TRUTH IS, WE HAVEN'T DATED STRAIGHT THROUGH UNDERGRAD and graduate school. There was a break after he cheated on me with one of his high school ex-girlfriends. That breakup was bad, but we somehow worked through it.

"YOUR LITTLE SECRET?" I PROP A HAND ON MY HIP. "FOREVER AND Always? Shit, Scott, I may be a fool believing there isn't something going on, but I'm not stupid."

"Dani..."

"Don't." I push him away. "You fucked your first cousin. You fucked her after sending me home. Because you said it wouldn't look good if I stayed over with her sleeping in the other room. You're a fucking tool, you know that?"

I FORGAVE HIM ONCE. EVERYTHING WAS PERFECT FOR A TIME.

Until it no longer was.

Fool me once, shame on you. Fool me twice, shame on me.

This is one hundred percent my fault for taking back a cheating asshole. It will never happen again. At least I found out before the wedding.

Another shudder ripples down my spine. What kind of life would that have been? Married to a man who cheats? And with his first cousin? Are there more women I don't know about? There was the girlfriend from high school. I find myself examining every interaction we've ever had.

I shake my head, incredulous. Shit like this doesn't happen in real life. Yet, here I am, staring into the eyes of an incestuous cheater.

"Dani, look, it's complicated. It's not like we planned it. It just happened."

"I doubt that. From the way you kept saying how gorgeous your cousin is and how you kept salivating over her in that dress, I have a hard time believing it just happened."

"It was just a little innocent kissing."

There was a time when I believed in love. Every little girl wants the fairytale to come true, a heroic knight, or prince, who swoops in to save the day. Scott was my fairytale. Now, he's nothing.

"You expect me to believe the two of you just kissed? I saw your apartment. You didn't sleep on the couch."

"The couch was uncomfortable."

"So you did what?" My voice rises. *"Crawled into bed, cuddled with your cousin, and your dick magically slipped between her legs?"*

A life with him would have been hell, and I'm thankful to find out before things go too far.

"That was the first and only time. I swear. It'll never happen again." His voice shakes, and he glances around the noisy common area of the student hall.

He's more concerned about other students hearing us argue than the fact I'm breaking up with him.

My last exam on Wednesday was a disaster. If the veterinary gods smile down on me, I might pull through and not fail the class. More tears the night before meant there was no last minute cramming for that exam.

Thankfully, I'm an A student. I won't flunk out of that class, although my standing among my peers will suffer. That affects my choice of clinical rotations for my fourth and final year.

Screw Scott.

No.

Beth can screw Scott.

I'm done with men.

Except Scott shows up on my doorstep after my exam, and then again the next morning. He isn't ready to let me go. Even after I return the ring, he tells me we need to talk. He'll fix everything. It will never happen again. He lies through his cheating teeth, desperate for me not to walk away.

Too little. Too late.

I never want to see him again.

Fuck Scott.

And thanks for Spring Break.

Many of my friends head off to tropical destinations, but not me. I miss my father, and my friends. Heading home to Bear Creek, trail rides on my daddy's ranch, and long nights beneath the stars are exactly what my broken heart needs to heal. I'll erase Scott from my memory and drown my sorrows in the crisp Montana air and skies that go on forever.

THREE

Dax

STILL EARLY IN THE AFTERNOON, DUSK COMES SWIFTLY TO THE SMALL town of Bear Creek. Nestled in the foothills of the northern edge of the Rocky Mountains, Bear Creek appears to be a quaint, quiet town. A place perfect for a man like me to catch my breath.

I pull into a spot in front of a cozy diner and turn off the ignition. A brightly painted sign outside welcomes everyone, but I hesitate. Instinct takes over, my heightened awareness has me scanning for threats.

The farther I drive from Egland Air Force Base, the more hyper-alert I become. Instead of my anxiety easing with each passing day, I feel adrift without my military family.

Abandoned and lost.

Not that I am.

My former teammates call me every day, helping pass the time as the miles pile up behind me on the road. They shoot the shit and keep me up to date on what they can. Mission details are classified, and I understand the distance that places between us.

They care.

They always will.

I'm the one with a problem, because I can't let go of my past or the career I trained a lifetime to have.

Time.

I have all the time in the world, and want none of it.

A quick look inside Marge's Diner reveals only a few patrons inside. That's good, as crowds are becoming more difficult to deal with as the days wear on. I get out of the truck and point a finger at Dynamo.

"You be good, boy."

To my surprise, there is a smaller sign on the door of the diner which says *All Dogs Welcome*. I turn around and let Dynamo jump out of the truck. His tail wags a mile a minute. His bright eyes stare up at me, full of adoration and absolute devotion.

"Looks like this is your lucky day." I tap the side of my leg and Dynamo pops into a perfect heel. We've only known each other a handful of days, and yet Dynamo surprises me with his intelligence. He's an easy dog. Hyper, but easy to travel with.

When I get around to it, I'll file official papers certifying Dynamo as a service dog. Then, I'll be able to keep Dynamo with me wherever I go. For now, I cope with crowds by staying as far away from other people as possible.

Three men sit around a table near the back of the diner. One of them is a Sheriff. They huddle over cups of steaming coffee and what looks to be some sort of pie. Barely past three pm, it seems an odd choice of both food and beverage.

A bright-eyed woman in her sixties appears to be in charge. She wears her hair in a loose bun and there's a crisp white apron wrapped around her waist. Immediately, she smiles at me. She reminds me of a fairy godmother.

Her smile is bright. Infectious. Her cheeks round. And her eyes sparkle, inviting me in.

She presides over the diner from behind an immaculate counter. When I walk in, she beams the most welcoming smile I've ever seen. The woman must have some fairy blood inside of her, because she works magic on me. My worries and fears melt away, my burdens lift, and I feel oddly at peace, almost as if I was coming home.

"Sit anywhere, hun. I'll be right with you." Her attention shifts to Dynamo and her eyes light up. "Oh, and I have treats for your dog, if that's okay?"

"Thank you, ma'am."

The three men glance up from their conversation, take one look at me, then go back to whatever they were discussing. I take a seat at the table by the window, as far from the men as possible.

The woman comes over with a menu tucked under her arm. "You want tea? Coffee? Water? Or something stronger? We've got beer and wine, but that's about it."

It feels too early to be drinking beer.

"I'll take some tea, please."

"Gotcha." She hands me the menu. "Everything is amazing. The pies are fresh, if you're looking for something sweet, and I'll bring over a bowl of water for your pup." She fishes out a dog biscuit from her pocket. "Is this okay?"

Dynamo lifts his head, nostrils flaring as he sniffs out the treat.

"Dynamo thanks you."

"Well, I'll get that tea and you figure out what you want. My name's Marge if you need anything." She leaves me to wipe dust off the empty tables and fuss over the men, refilling their coffee and talking with them.

When Marge returns, I order a burger and fries. A woman with a bubbly personality, Marge seems to get the hint I'm not up for conversation and leaves me to stew in silence.

I'm deep in thought about the direction of my life. On terminal leave from the military, I still have a paycheck coming in, however, it'll be a few months, maybe a year, before my VA check kicks in. That means, I need to find work, or find my way home.

I'm not ready for that.

Not yet.

Which means I need a job.

But who will hire a stranger in a place like this? What kind of job do I want?

Nothing that ties me down, but something which allows me to put a roof over my head, food in my belly, and a warm place for Dynamo to sleep.

Highly attuned to my surroundings at all times, the conversation of the men behind me drifts to my ears.

"I've got a boom on calves, a shortage of good men, and too many excuses from those I have." A man with a blue baseball cap pushes his steaming coffee toward the center of the table and hunches over the remnants of his apple pie.

"Hire more hands." The Sheriff takes a swig of coffee. His attention shifts to me, and I give a curt nod after a thorough once over.

"I would, except there seems to be a shortage of men who know how to handle themselves on a ranch, let alone during calving season."

My ears perk up at the men's conversation.

"Have you tried online?"

"Waste of my time. Get a bunch of freaks thinking the work will be easy and the pay better than it is. I swear, no one is willing to work hard these days, and nobody is willing to hire on for the short term. Any that do know nothing about cattle. By the time I train them, I won't need them any longer, and I don't have time to hold their hands, or put them in a saddle."

I debate what to do when Marge brings my meal. She places a bowl of wet dog food on the floor for Dynamo.

"Thank you ma'am."

"Anytime."

"You're a dog lover I take it?" I look for an opening with Marge. I sense she has her finger on the pulse of the local community.

"Guilty," she flashes a grin. "I hate when people have to leave their dogs tied up outside. As long as they're well behaved, they're welcome here."

"The dogs or the people?" I wink at her and return her friendly smile.

Marge's laughter warms my heart. Genuine and unencumbered, it's a wonderful sound for a tired soul.

"Both." Her eyes glimmer with laughter.

I hook my thumb over my shoulder. "How about them? Do they fall in the well-behaved crowd?"

She flaps the rag she uses to clean the tables. "Tom and Jerry are good men, and Sheriff Johnson isn't so bad."

"Thank you." It's not much of an endorsement, but everything I need.

When she leaves my table, I tie the end of Dynamo's leash to the table leg. We're working on basic commands when not in the truck, and while incredibly smart and attentive, we're still working out the kinks of who's in charge.

I take a bite of my food, then devour the entire burger in just a few bites. Wiping my chin, I decide to take a leap of faith.

My chair scrapes over the linoleum and I wander over to the men.

"Couldn't help but overhear, and sorry to intrude, but did I hear you're looking for an extra hand?"

The man in the ball cap sizes me up. His eyes widen and I know exactly what the man thinks. Men don't develop my kind of physique if they're afraid of hard labor. I have what this man needs, and more. Lucky day for the both of us, if it works out.

"You know anything about ranching?"

"I know a thing or two." I keep my answers short, not divulging too much information. I don't want these men to know my link to Texas and Kingston Ranch.

I grew up on Texas's largest cattle ranch. The business flows in my veins, but it wasn't enough to keep me home, much to my father's chagrin.

That's just one thing in a long list of disappointments.

Seth Kingston's only son walked away from a cattle empire, and he never lets me forget it. But, I didn't want to manage cattle for a living. I wanted to save lives and make a difference in the world, not spend it eating dust with heifers, bulls, and calves.

Calving season can be rough. It depends on the size of the herd, and the man in the ball cap looked stressed. We're going to help each other out.

"It's calving season, son. Do you know what that means?"

"Long days and longer nights. If you need an extra hand, I can help." I point to my dog. "Dynamo is a young dog, and if you don't mind, he'd be a great help too."

"A Blue Heeler. Impressive. Is he trained?"

"Not yet. He's a rescue dog, believe it or not, but he's learning."

The man exchanges a look with his friends. He crosses his arms over his chest. "You got references?"

"Just separated from the Air Force. I can have my commander drop you a line."

"How about your skills? Know how to ride a horse?"

"Born in the saddle." I cock my head.

"Rope a bull?"

"Easy as pie."

I perfected my rope skills before I was ten. Roping a bull isn't hard. It's those dang calves once they get their legs under them that are difficult. Bastards love to run and can cut on a dime.

"Know anything about calving?"

"Yes, sir. Cut out the heavies and put them near the calving shed. Rinse and repeat every few days, and always remember that whatever can go wrong will. Let the cows do their thing. They don't need no help, except when they do. Then it's the chain and calf puller to help her out."

The man huffs a laugh. "Sounds like you have experience."

"You tell me where and when and I'll prove my worth. But head's up, I'm not looking for anything permanent. I just got out of the Air Force and I'm not looking to settle down. Just need something to pass the time. Will that be a problem?"

"No, that would work out fine. It doesn't pay much. The days are long…"

"And the nights longer." I finish the man's sentence. Anyone who knows anything about calving season knows it's a 24/7 operation until the last calf is born.

"You'll get a fair wage, food and board. Paid in cash."

"As long as my dog is welcome, that sounds fine to me."

His eyes narrow. "You a wanted man?"

"No sir."

"Done anything you shouldn't?"

"Every man has, but nothing that would put me behind bars. Look, I served my country, but now she's done with me. All I need is a little space and some breathing room to figure out my next step. I'm not looking for trouble, but can handle it if it comes."

I don't know the Montana cattle scene. Kingston Ranch is big enough we don't have to worry about poaching and thieving. Things might be different around here.

"Our trouble comes in the four-footed variety, wolves, coyotes, and the occasional mountain lion. You good with a gun?"

"I've been known to hit a barn door." I'm an expert marksman and can hit a dime at a thousand yards. "If the work is honest, I don't mind if it's hard."

"The work is hard, but you seem to know that. You up for it?"

"Yes sir."

The man gives me a long appraising look, then finishes with a sharp nod. "I think I can help with that." The man stands and stretches out his hand. "Name's Tom Studer. I own Crowbar Ranch and a few hundred head of cattle."

That's nothing compared to the tens of thousands cattle at Kingston Ranch. This will be good.

Hard work is exactly the distraction I need to get over the mess going on in my head.

FOUR

Dani

THE DRIVE FROM PULLMAN TO BEAR CREEK TAKES A FEW HOURS. Nothing is close out west and I have to pass through the northern part of Idaho before heading into the rugged mountains near home.

Around each twist and turn, amazing views greet me with sweeping vistas. As the miles pile behind me, I breathe easier and my tears dry up. The mountains will always be home to me, providing comfort and respite. It's the same with the pastures which nestle at the foot of mountains. I'm a country girl through and through.

As I descend down the steep roads, the distant plains spread out before me, extending their welcome home.

My father will be upset about Scott, and I don't know if I'll be able to keep him from seeking revenge against Scott for breaking his little girl's heart. My father's overprotectiveness was impossible to deal with growing up, but I appreciate every bit of it now.

A tear slips free.

Will I ever be free of the pain Scott leaves behind?

Time heals all wounds.

Some idiot thought that up, because I don't think there will ever be a time when the pain goes away. Scott drove a spike through my heart and it hurts like hell.

A few miles out from town, a low *thump, thump, thump* sounds and the whole car vibrates.

Just what I need.

Fortunately, my father taught me how to change a flat and perform basic maintenance on my vehicle. Not that I'm a mechanic. Not by any stretch of the imagination. But I know what a dipstick is and how to use it. I can also change a flat.

There's little traffic on the road. Nonetheless, I remember my father's words about pulling off to the side. The shoulder can be the most dangerous place for a motorist. Tired drivers often zone in on the brake lights of parked cars pulled off to the side, and plow right into the parked car.

It's still early in the day, but I heed my father's words and pull as far off the shoulder as I can. At least it isn't hot.

My friends might be enjoying tropical temperatures on the beaches in the Caribbean, but in Montana, springtime means chilly temperatures and the occasional snow. Fortunately, the roads are clear, and it's warm enough to trick the wildflowers into bloom.

A definite chill hangs in the air. At least it isn't bitingly cold. I shrug out of my jacket and get to work.

Sure enough, my rear driver's side tire is flat. A quick inspection reveals a nail sticking through the sidewall. Not something I can patch and re-inflate. Fortunately, my Jeep has a full-sized spare.

I bend down to loosen the lug nuts. Placing the tire iron over the nuts, I give a hard yank.

Nothing.

I try again.

The lug nut refuses to budge.

That's okay. My father taught me how to use leverage to my advantage.

When that fails to crack any of the lug nuts loose I hop up and down on the end of the tire iron. Still nothing. Not a single one of the lug nuts moves. I finally accept defeat and pull out my cell phone.

Only, there's no service.

In the mountains, cell coverage is spotty at best. Just my luck, I manage to break down in a dead zone.

The rumble of a truck engine sounds behind me and I glance up at a beat-up pickup truck approaching. Most people in these places are good people, but I trust no one.

Hoping the truck keeps going, I grip my phone. When it slows, I edge to the driver's side door. I keep a firearm stored under my seat and unlock the combination to the box while the truck pulls in front of my vehicle and comes to a stop.

I stand there, using the driver's door as a shield, one hand on the frame and the other primed to grab my gun as the front door of the truck opens.

A dog jumps out followed by the slow stretch of a man's leg. He wears boots and worn jeans. When he stands, he keeps getting taller and taller and oh my, he's big. Big, tall, and full of muscles bunching on top of more muscles.

Things can go south quickly if his intent isn't friendly. I reach down and palm my gun. A quick check confirms the safety's engaged. I leave it on for now. If I have to shoot, I can disengage it and hit the man square in the chest from where he stands, four car lengths away.

Taller than the average man, he must be well over six feet tall. His muscular definition points to a man who isn't afraid of hard work.

My father would appreciate such a thing. He always complains about how difficult it is to find good workers for the ranch.

If I were in Pullman, I'd think this man lived in the gym and survived by guzzling protein shakes, but out here he probably earned that physique from hard, honest work.

Only, there's a caginess about him that isn't present in bone-weary ranch hands. He reminds me of a predator who recently found freedom. Like he doesn't know whether to run or bite the closest thing to him. Right now, the closest thing is me, and I refuse to become a rape statistic.

I grip my gun and press my thumb beside the safety. In a heartbeat, I can shoot.

He closes the distance in ground-devouring strides. His boots crunch on the gravel as he draws near. But he stops several paces away. His eyes narrow and he cocks his head.

"You need help, miss?"

"I'm good. Thank you." I'll hike until I find cell reception. That seems safer than spending any more time with this man alone. And what a man he is, all feral and wild. Delicious and captivating, he draws me to him. There's something about him. Maybe it's the blaze blue of his eyes? Or the sharpness of his jaw? Or the flex of his broad hand and all the veins popping out along his forearms?

Maybe it's the long jagged scar running down the side of his face?

He runs long fingers through his short-cropped brown hair. There's a little length on top, which shifts back into place once his hand goes past. The man's rugged jawline bunches as he grits his teeth.

"You sure about that?" He glances at the flat tire. "Looks like you could use some help."

"I know how to change a flat, thank you very much."

His brows climb up his forehead and he takes a step back. "I wasn't questioning your abilities, but rather offering a hand."

His square jaw and high cheekbones perfectly accentuate his face. An unusual combination, it makes him insanely attractive, or maybe it's the long diagonal scar running from the tip of his eye to the corner of his mouth that speaks of danger. Whatever injury caused it, the pink, puckered skin speaks to something recent. And it says in no uncertain terms this man is dangerous.

It's something I should listen to, but I don't find myself running away. Instead, it makes me all the more curious.

He cups his cheek when he notices the direction of my gaze.

"I'm sorry. I didn't mean to stare."

"Don't be. You want help or not?" He glances overhead, looking bored.

I need help, but am too full of pride to admit I can't do it myself. Why is it so hard to smile and be thankful for his help?

Because of Scott.

My hatred of all men is the reason. Douchebag Scott turned me into a raving bitch who can't accept help from a stranger. I roll my eyes and take a deep breath. This stranger doesn't deserve my anger.

"I tried loosening the lug nuts, but they're frozen."

"Mind if I give it a go?"

"Be my guest." I grip the frame of the door, tensing.

"Mind putting down the weapon?"

"How did you...?"

He cocks his head and the corner of his mouth lifts into a grin. The smile transforms his face into the most amazing thing I've ever seen, softening the garish scar, and revealing something of the man underneath. His lightly tanned skin glows. Men around here don't develop their tans until late spring, which means...

"You're not from around here, are you?"

"What makes you say that?" His full, pink lips press firmly together and his brows draw tight.

"Just a feeling."

He takes a long look at me, his gaze sweeping from head to toe. Despite the thoroughness of the assessment, I don't feel threatened. It isn't like he's checking me out, but rather making a list of my strengths and weaknesses. Whatever he decides, I seem to pass some test.

"You're not either." When he crosses his arms over his chest, the muscles of his biceps flex, drawing my attention once again to his impressive physique.

"Actually, I am. I grew up here."

"Here?"

"Yes, here." I shouldn't give out personal information, but I can't help the words spewing from my mouth. "Just on the other side of the mountains."

"Bear Creek?"

"You're familiar with it?"

"In fact, I am. But you don't live there." His eyes pinch together. "I'm guessing college kid? Coming home on break?"

I don't know why my mouth keeps working, because I have nothing to prove to this man.

"I'm not a kid."

This time, the sweep of his gaze lingers on my breasts and dips lower to stare at the juncture of my legs.

"I'm well aware of that, but you still have a problem."

"What's that?"

He points to the flat. "Look, we can talk all day, but this is my day off, and I'd rather not spend it on the side of the road. I promised Dynamo a run on the trails."

I notice how he doesn't say hike, but rather run. Looking at him, I imagine he can run miles on the mountain trails. His dog sniffs at the bushes leading into the trees, but his ears perk up at the mention of his name. Dynamo trots over to the stranger, sniffs the man's hand, and licks his fingers before heading back to investigate the bushes again.

The man points to the tire. "If you put away your weapon, I'll lend a hand."

He keeps calling my gun a weapon.

"Are you military?"

"Not anymore."

Well, that answers that.

"How did you know I had a gun?"

"Lucky guess, but you're awfully twitchy, telegraphing your every thought. You should work on that. Do you even know how to shoot that thing?" His brow arches and my temper flares at the insinuation I don't know how to shoot.

"I know how to shoot."

"Knowing how to shoot and actually hitting something are two different things."

"You think because I'm a woman I can't hit anything?"

He holds up his hands. "I didn't say shit about you being a woman. You brought that into this. Not me."

I don't believe him. All men think women can't shoot. I'm a damn good shot, but I still don't know how he knows I have a gun. It wasn't a guess, either.

He knew.

Much to my chagrin, the man gets better looking the more I stare at him. I really shouldn't stare, except there's simply too much of him to admire.

He runs his hand through his hair again.

"Look, I can go..." He pivots toward his truck.

"No," I say, blurting out the word.

As much as I hate asking for help when I should be able to take care of things, the simple truth is that I need it.

"You sure?" A cocky grin fills his face. The bastard is having fun with me. "I wouldn't want to assume a woman can't change a simple tire."

His eyes will be my undoing. They're deep and catastrophic, the kind of eyes a girl can get lost in. A vivid baby blue they melt my resolve to not give in to his devilishly handsome good looks.

"I'm sure."

He holds his hands out. "Secure that weapon and I'll reconsider helping you."

"What do you mean reconsider? You wouldn't leave me here?"

"A strong, independent woman like you? Sure as shit I'd leave your ass."

"You're a real bastard, you know that?"

"I'm also strong enough to loosen those lug nuts, and it's rude to insult a stranger."

"Fine." I secure the gun, locking it in place, and step away from the Jeep. "Thank you for stopping."

"My pleasure." He flashes me a grin and closes the distance.

Up close, I'm overcome by the overwhelming maleness of him, raw and potent, I don't like the way my heart races or my blood pounds in my veins.

He bends a knee and loosens the lug nuts with barely any effort. Then he stands and hands me the tire iron.

"I assume you know how to jack up your Jeep, change the wheel, and tighten everything down again?"

I lift my chin. "Yes. Of course I do."

"Well, good luck then." He starts to walk away.

"Aren't you going to finish changing the tire?"

Damn if he doesn't have dimples, too. Although, the scar hides the one on the left side of his face.

"And deprive you of your independence? Hell no. Have a nice day, and be wary of strangers. You never know who you can trust."

Now, why did he say that?

I ball my hands into fists when he whistles to the dog. Dynamo bounds over the grass and into the truck. The man climbs in and shuts the door. A second later, the engine cranks over and he drives away.

"What the ever-loving hell just happened?"

Half an hour later, I tighten the last of the lug nuts. I would've been done much sooner, except I had problems getting the jack to work. Elbow grease spent, two bruised knuckles later, and I get it to work. If that man stayed, I wouldn't have broken a nail.

And damn if I don't know his name.

FIVE

Dax

EXCEPT FOR THE MOUNTAINS, IT'S HARD NOT TO FEEL LIKE I'M home.

Down from Bear Creek, rolling plains extend as far as the eye can see. Cattle graze much of the land, but there's still a good portion used for crops. Oil and natural gas operations make up the rest, but not nearly on the scale as that of Texas.

But then, Texas always does things bigger and better than everyone else.

Rich, untapped oil reserves sit below much of Montana land. Once the cost of bringing that oil to the surface becomes profitable, the area will experience a boom similar to what Texas experienced. For now, rolling pastureland extends out from the base of the mountains relatively untouched by oil rigs and fracking operations.

I know about both.

My family's land has rich oil deposits, and while our business is primarily that of cattle, a good chunk of our profits come from the oil and natural gas found beneath Kingston land.

Despite the difficulties I have with my father, I can't say Seth Kingston neglected his son growing up. From the day I learned to ride, my father kept me by his side, teaching me everything about cattle, ranching, and drilling for oil.

A conservationist, my father taught about the fine balance that needs to be maintained so as not to ruin the land. A tough bastard, my father made sure I knew everything about the family business so that I can step in at any time and take over.

Not that I want to.

Perhaps that's why my decision to enlist in the military came as such a shock, and met with intense resistance and downright hostility. Seth Kingston thought I was wasting my time screwing around in the military while putting my life at risk for no reason. As the only son to inherit Kingston lands, and the rich oil which flows beneath it, this figured prominently on my father's mind.

Long ago, I agreed to disagree with my father about that.

Dynamo licks the passenger side window and I shake my head. I gave up trying to keep the glass clean by our third day together.

"You think this is a good place to pull over?" I scan the small scenic overlook and stop the truck without waiting on Dynamo's approval.

Spending the day by the side of the highway is not the plan.

My first day off since starting work on Old Man Studer's ranch, I promised Dynamo a long, overland run through the mountains. I miss the intense burn a long cross country run brings. Hell, I miss much about my previous life; morning PT being only one of many things.

Studer has me up and in the saddle from five in the morning until well past sunset. It took less than a day to figure out Studer's operation, and from the nod he gave me, I figure Studer thought it would take much longer. My aptitude and skill is a surprise to the man.

I keep my replies short when Studer asks how I know as much as I do about cattle, saying only that I grew up working on a ranch. Everything else is immaterial and I'm not looking to bond with the man. This is a short-lived gig, and in a few weeks, I'll move on. I haven't really decided what to do next.

"We may not get in that hike, 'Mo, if that girl doesn't hurry up and change her damn tire." I turn to the dog who goes to town licking his balls. "Dude!" I turn away and look back the way we came.

The girl was cagey and nervous, palming a small pistol when I stopped to help. Then she did the unthinkable. She knocked me off my game.

My reaction makes no sense, because it's not like me to leave a woman stranded who needs help.

Although, I didn't really leave her stranded. Those lug nuts are loose enough for her to remove, and she was pretty snarky about her ability to change a tire. Regardless, I left her on the side of the road with the job unfinished. But I wait here to make sure she's okay.

That makes me half a hero.

I intentionally left her, if only because I want to see what she'll do.

That makes me a full on asshole.

I snicker at that.

Full of spitfire and something I can't describe, the flare of her temper makes my blood race and my body take notice. I was hard from the first moment I saw her.

"You think I should've finished the job?" I glance over at Dynamo looking for absolution.

Dynamo gives me a look, then goes back to licking his balls.

My mother will have a fit if she ever finds out her son left a woman on the side of the road, but damn if I can't help myself. I had every intention of changing out the tire, but that girl pushed my buttons in the strangest way.

Girl?

Woman?

She's a few years younger than me, early twenties maybe? Most definitely not a girl.

Whatever.

It doesn't matter.

It's enough that I can't ignore the difference in our ages. In my early thirties, she is still a kid to me, but damn what a figure she cuts with her perky tits, narrow waist, tight ass and toned thighs. Every man's wet dream, my fantasies will be full of her through the long nights ahead.

"Probably a good thing we didn't exchange names. Right 'Mo?"

Dynamo kicks his rear foot up in the air and scratches behind his ear.

Barely legal, it's best if I stay far away from the girl.

I still don't know what to think about the pounding in my veins, the hitch of my breath, or the way her doe-brown eyes made my gut twist in knots. I'm most certainly not going to acknowledge what happened to my dick. The bastard took one look at the girl and stood up in stiff salute.

The thoughts churning in my head keep my dick hard, thoughts which would rightfully earn me a shot from that gun of hers. Which means, I need to leave her to her business and drive away.

Tapping my thumb on the steering wheel, I consider doing just that for about half a second. The truth is, I need another look at her, and if she doesn't drive around that curve soon, I'll turn back and make sure everything is okay.

What if someone else stops to help her? What if someone with unsavory intentions sees the girl as easy prey?

I hate to think of any woman having to worry about her safety when stranded by the side of the road. The sad truth is not everyone is like me. At least I had the good sense to walk away when my body said to do exactly the opposite.

So Others Might Live might be the motto of a Para Jumper, and while I believe every word, I also believe another more profound saying.

Protect and Serve.

Dynamo gives a tiny whine and paws at the door latch. The damn dog is too smart. I don't put it past him to open the door and get a head start on that run I promised.

"Just a little longer." I reach out and scratch between Dynamo's ears. "We'll give her time."

I could've changed the tire in less than five minutes. I cringe thinking about leaving her to do it all by herself. It's kind of an asshole move.

With nothing but time to kill while I wait for her Jeep to appear around the bend, my thoughts drift to the town of Bear Creek and its sister town Peace Springs.

I've learned a few things about some of the more colorful characters in town. Between Marge and Tom Studer, I know far more than I want.

An older man, Bert, runs a llama ranch. He sells the hair, which makes sense, but it's the use of the llamas as therapy animals which catches my interest. Not that I need a therapy animal.

Dynamo does just fine in that category, and as long as I stay away from the larger towns, that itchy anxiety stays away. But it's cool the way Bert's llamas help autistic children, and others with special needs. I might mention it to my father, a sort of public service Kingston Ranch can provide to our community.

Studer gave me a run down on the other ranches in the area. There are two operations I want to check out, if only because of the men who run them. The special ops community isn't that big. To find not one but two men within a days drive who worked within the same circles while in the military intrigues me. Drake is an ex-Green Beret. Caleb is a Marine and former Delta Operative whom I know from the few missions we ran together, back in the day.

It's not uncommon for Air Force PJs to be assigned to our sister services. I worked with the SEALs several times, but it's the missions with Delta Force that were the most fun. I never worked with the Green Berets and consider that a loss.

Intense rivalry exists within the special ops teams. SEALS get all the press, and women tend to lose their ever-loving minds if they think they have a chance to bag a SEAL.

The Green Berets tease that SEAL stands for Sleep Eat and Lift, an insult of the worst kind, but given because that's all SEALs do while training for their short, micro missions. The Green Berets, on the other hand, embed for months at a time with zero support. And they don't get all the hero worship lavished on the SEALs.

I tend to stay out of the whole rivalry thing.

Once things settle down on Crowbar ranch, I'll take a minute to check in on Caleb Caswell. Until then, my days are busy. Mid-spring, calving season is still a week away which gives me a couple of days to get comfortable with Studer's operation.

I survey the small herd with the old man, pointing out the cows closest to dropping their calves. Called *heavies*, they need to be separated from the main herd and moved to a smaller pasture nearest the barn.

The first few days were a test of my capabilities. I must have passed, or impressed my new boss, because Studer didn't accompany me these last two days, trusting my ability to identify appropriate heavies to separate.

During calving season, we'll repeat the process several times, as mothers less far along in gestation come closer to their time of delivery. Not that everything makes sense to me. I ask about the timing of the season as it is several weeks later than what we do on Kingston Ranch.

Spring in Texas brings rain, heat, and humidity, and our cows calve in late January rather than mid-spring. People think breeding is random and unpredictable, but exactly the opposite is true. An astute rancher can limit calving to within a month's period of time by properly managing his bulls and their access to the herd.

I finally understand the reason behind the later calving season when the first cold snap arrives three days after I come to town.

My first day in Bear Creek it was in the mid-fifties. I didn't think much of it and looked forward to hard work without a blazing sun scorching the earth and searing my skin. The next two days, the temperatures dropped to the teens and three inches of snow fell. That kind of shit doesn't happen in Texas.

Studer says it can get much worse. Snow seems to love Montana.

And it kind of makes sense to delay calving until the threat of blizzards passes. Studer tells me it isn't unusual to have a blizzard in May. Just a few years back, two feet of snow dropped over a span of six hours.

That isn't good for newly born calves, wet with amniotic fluid, who struggle to stand, let alone nurse at their mother's teats.

In Texas, we split our calving season in two, late January and early summer. It makes sense on a ranch managing tens of thousands of cattle. Calving takes non-stop work until the last cow drops her calf. Also, it spreads out the other end of that burden when we take yearlings to market for slaughter.

Deep in my thoughts, the low drone of a vehicle has me snapping up straight. I'm not one to let my guard down. That should bother me, but I find myself relaxing when I see who turns the corner.

It's the girl in her Jeep.

I watch as she drives around the bend and tip my hat when she looks over at my truck. An old beat up monstrosity, it's nothing to look at but hasn't failed me yet. The urge to follow has my hand on the keys before I realize what I'm doing.

There's no way I should follow the girl, but my gut tells me I need to make sure she makes it to her destination safely. A man following a girl after helping her beside the road is creepy as shit, but I turn the key. Tires spitting gravel, I pull onto the road.

I reach across the seat and tug on Dynamo's collar.

"Sorry, boy. No run today."

Wounded. Battle-scarred. My life was irreparably altered in service to my country, but I don't regret it. I can't believe my father may have been right.

The stabbing pain in my chest when the girl looks at me is something ferocious, a deep-seated ache I don't understand. When her expression didn't turn to revulsion at the scar on my face, I know I'm more than a wounded vet who has been used up.

That girl sees the man beneath the scar and I need to know what that means.

My parents fell in love at first sight, and I always thought I would follow in their footsteps, but the love bug never hit me. Except the moment I laid eyes on the girl with the Jeep, something fundamental shifted within my chest.

SIX

Dani
———————

I can't tell if the flutter in my belly is that of righteous anger or something else. When I see the truck parked beside the road, and the fierce stare of its occupant as I drive by, several choice curse words escape my mouth.

If that bastard has enough time to sit by the road, why did he leave me to change the flat by myself?

Not that I was particularly nice to him, but still.

What happened to chivalry?

Is it true all the good men are gone?

They certainly aren't around here, and they most certainly aren't back in Pullman with dickwad Scott.

Perhaps it's a good thing my stranger didn't stick around. Although, he's drool worthy and worth a second look. I literally spent the last hour trying to get him out of my thoughts, which proved impossible.

I have half a mind to stop and tell him exactly what I think, but by the time I work up my courage, I've already passed him by.

Sitting by the side of the road?

Like he has nothing better to do than waste his time?

I broke two nails and have a gash on my knuckle. Tires are heavy!

Bastard.

The muscles in my hands ache from gripping the steering wheel as I crank through the twists and turns and head down the winding road. The highway descends gradually, weaving relentlessly toward Bear Creek. The shadows cast by the peaks and ridges lengthen as the sun slips behind their craggy peaks.

When I finally drive into Bear Creek, I pull in opposite Marge's Diner. No one comes to town without stopping in to see Marge first. When I hop out of the vehicle, a huge grin splits my face when I see who's inside.

The bell over the door gives a little jingle as I push it open.

"Cate!" My squeal has my best friend lifting her head, and her massive dog, Bear, looks up with a slow, lazy blink. It's the only acknowledgment the Newfoundland gives that someone entered. He may look like a lazy thing, but there's an incredible powerhouse hidden within the massive animal.

"Dani?" Cate's eyes widen. "Why didn't you tell me you were coming home early? We weren't expecting you until Saturday."

"Welcome home." Marge beams her signature smile and wraps me in a hug. Cate and I always joke about how Marge reminds us of the blue fairy godmother from Sleeping Beauty.

"My midterms were over and there wasn't a reason to stay." I shrug and try to keep the heartache from my voice, not wanting to ruin what should be a happy reunion. My love life is a disaster and I don't want to talk about it.

"What about Scott?" Cate's eyebrows lift. "Where's he?"

Cate is arguably my best friend in the whole world. We've known each other since we were babies, went to the same grade school, middle school, and high school. With a class of less than fifty kids, we all formed a tight, indelible bond.

I press my lips together. It's not necessary to say anything. With one look, Cate knows. We have a spooky connection like that. Always have.

"What happened?" Cate pulls me to the table she's sitting at and waves at Marge. "Coffee and apple pie, STAT! And an extra scoop of ice cream."

Marge wipes her hands on her apron and gives me a motherly look which says two things. First, she's sorry, and second, things will get better.

"I thought everything was going well? You said he proposed." Cate glances at my hand. "What happened?"

I let a deep sigh slip out. While my arrival got no initial reaction out of Bear, he lifts his muzzle and licks my hand, sensing my emotional distress. I absently reach down and thread my fingers through his thick fur.

"He cheated on me."

"Oh, you poor dear." Marge brings over a cup of coffee and fills Cate's half empty cup. Placing the pot on the table, she pulls me into another hug.

"With his first cousin." It hurts to say it out loud. I feel foolish and ashamed. That makes me mad, because I did nothing wrong. There's nothing for me to be ashamed about.

"Holy crap balls! That sucks." Cate reaches out and threads her fingers through mine. "I'm so sorry. Want me to get my shotgun?"

I laugh. I can always count on Cate to lighten the mood. I wipe the tears from my cheeks.

"If it wasn't against the law, I'd say give me the gun."

"I'm a better shot than you. We each get one, and we make him suffer."

A smile slips past my lips and I find myself laughing with my best friend as we go through a hundred different ways to make Scott pay.

Marge brings over the pie, along with three scoops of ice cream. "He slept with his first cousin?"

"Yeah."

"That's a whole other level of wrong. You dodged a bullet, girl." Marge sits with us while we dig in. "Don't worry about Scott." Marge shovels a bite of pie into her mouth and waves the spoon in the air. "He did you a favor. At least you found out what kind of man he is before you tied yourself to him."

"I know." I sit back and cross my ankles. "Dad is going to be upset. He really liked Scott."

"I'm sure he did." Cate scoops up some of the vanilla ice cream. "But when he finds out what Scott did to his little girl, we'll be the ones holding him back from the gun case."

"You're probably right about that." My father is known to be overprotective of his little girl. "Do you remember what he did to Brent?"

Brent Calloway went to high school with us. We ran in the same small circle and he asked me to go to Prom with him.

On Prom night, my father waited on the front porch with a shot gun balanced across his lap.

"Oh, yes!" Cate squealed. "Brent talked about that for weeks!"

Fortunately, Brent brought me home with ten minutes to spare. I don't have cool stories about Prom, or any other night because I didn't date in high school. My father didn't allow it.

Brent and I were nothing more than good friends. We both wanted to go to Prom, and neither of us was seeing anyone. My father reluctantly agreed to allow me to go with Brent, but it came with a threat of bodily harm and buckshot to Brent's ass if he brought me home a minute past curfew. We had the best time that night.

"Speaking of Brent…" Cate leans in close and lowers her voice to a whisper. "I've got news."

We move past the ugliness of Scott's betrayal as Cate tells me about Brent and the girl he intends to marry. At least he found his happily ever after. Cate did too. It seems my friends are all on their way to finding their happily ever afters.

The three of us catch up on all the local town gossip, which means Marge talks while Cate and I listen. Bear falls back asleep, content to lean against our legs.

"I forgot to ask about Bear," I blurt out. "How's he doing?"

Bear was injured in a cougar attack not too long ago. Cate was involved in a mountain rescue of a couple of college kids and Bear saved her life.

That occurred around the time Caleb finally got his head out of his ass and came back to Bear Creek. Cate and Caleb were high school sweethearts and everyone thought they'd get married, but that didn't happen. Caleb left to join the Marines, leaving Cate behind, at least until he finally came home. It took over seven years, but Cate and Caleb finally found each other.

Cate and now Brent?

Will I be the only one from our high school class who never finds my soulmate?

Another deep sigh escapes my lips.

"Bear is doing just fine," Cate says. "You can't even tell he was hurt."

"I'm really glad he's doing so well." I reach down and rub Bear's shoulder.

"Speaking of..." Cate says, "have you given any thought as to what kind of vet you're going to be? Large animal or small? And do you have your clerkships picked out for next year?"

"I haven't really decided, and no. We don't pick our clerkships for the final year until after midterms. Based on ranking, we'll have to see what I get."

"You're top of your class. I'm sure you'll have first pick. Draven is looking for a partner down in Peace Springs. You should ask to see if he would let you work with him. Wouldn't that be great?"

"It would, but I don't know if he's approved as a clerkship site. And I don't know about having my pick. Scott kind of messed all that up." My voice cracks. "I couldn't think and basically cried my way through my exams. I'll be surprised if I pass. I don't know what I'm going to do when I have to go back and see him again."

Cate takes my hand in hers again. "Girl, you don't have to do anything, and Scott doesn't deserve one more second of your time, your thoughts, or your tears."

"I thought he was the one." I can't help the flood of tears, and wipe at my cheeks. Scott was supposed to have been my forever.

"Hun," Marge says, "he's the one you needed before you could find the one you want. Don't give up on love. It's out there, just waiting to bite you when you least expect it."

I wish I had Marge's faith, but the truth is I remain unlucky in love. I gave Scott the last seven years of my life. While I don't need a man, it was always part of my life's plan.

College.

Vet school.

Marriage.

Kids.

Now, I only see the first two of those happening. Bear Creek is small. Peace Springs isn't much bigger. If a girl doesn't find her man right out of high school around here, her chances of landing one plummet.

"All that time wasted…" Anger heats my cheeks and I blow out my breath.

"You're being overly melodramatic." Cate kicks me in the shin.

"Ow! That hurts."

"It wasn't supposed to tickle. I know exactly what you're thinking."

"No, you don't."

"Dani's life plan…" Cate lifts her hand and begins ticking off each finger. "College. Vet school. Marriage…"

"It's not a stupid list."

"Never said it was stupid, but you're acting like your life is over because some asshat cheated on you. You're an incredibly successful woman and your entire life is ahead of you. Just because Scott was a douche doesn't mean Mr. Right isn't out there waiting for you." She points over my shoulder toward the window. "Like, hello gorgeous. Who the hell is that?"

Marge turns to look where Cate points and her cheeks round with a smile and her eyes twinkle. "That is a very handsome stranger who's new in town. You should talk to him, Dani. Give him the Bear Creek welcome."

I huff and refuse to look. "I'm not interested in a rebound man."

Cate points again. "Seriously Dani, turn around. A man who can wear a pair of jeans like that deserves to be appreciated."

"Won't Caleb be pissed you're ogling another man?"

"Caleb knows my heart is his, but I'm not blind. Now, seriously, turn around and take a look."

I give another huff. They aren't letting me get out of this, and what will it matter if I admire an attractive man? Slowly, I shift, making sure I don't accidentally disturb the snoozing Bear as I move my feet. When I finally manage to twist around, my jaw drops.

"Yeah," Cate says. "That is one sexy man."

No denying it. I fantasized about him the entire drive down into Bear Creek.

A man doesn't sculpt a body like that overnight. He spends a lifetime picking up heavy objects, putting them down, and repeating the action a million times. My breath catches when my stranger opens the passenger door of his beat up pick up. A blue speckled heeler jumps out and hops around his legs.

"That man is a tool." I cross my arms over my chest. "Total tool."

"What?" Cate's head whips around, then swivels back to take in the man who appears to be walking toward Marge's Diner. "Why would you say that?"

I briefly relay my encounter by the side of the road. Cate's eyes round but Marge merely smiles as she stands and presses out the wrinkles of her apron. Her gaze shifts between me and the stranger and she laughs under her breath.

The man strolls into Marge's looking like he owns the place. There's a presence about him, a confidence which oozes from his pores and forces everyone in attendance to take notice.

I despise him because I do exactly that. I can't stop looking at him.

He glances around the small diner, sweeping the room with his astute gaze, and our eyes meet for a split second. While I blush beneath the intensity of his tight focus, his lips curl into a smile. Then the most infuriating thing happens. Instead of acknowledging me, he lets the sweep of his gaze move on.

I'm not sure if he mocks me, ignores me, or is just being a dick.

The dog trots beside him and sits when he comes to a stop behind Marge's counter.

"Dynamo claims he's starving." The deep rumble of his voice makes the air vibrate and sends a shiver racing down my spine. "Do you have one of your treats for him?"

"Of course." Marge turns to her stash of dog treats and opens the tin can. Bear's nostrils flare and he lifts his head. "I'm getting one for you too, Bear. I swear these dogs are spoiled."

"By the most amazing woman on the planet." The man takes the dog biscuit and tosses it in the air. Dynamo snaps it up before it hits the ground and goes to town chomping on the treat.

"Can I get you something? Pie? Coffee? Beer?" Marge keeps glancing between me and the stranger, a mischievous light flickering in her eyes. "You haven't been around the last couple days."

My stranger glances over at me and I feel every lick of his heated gaze.

"I was busy today. Missed out on a run with Dynamo."

"How's that?"

"I had to stop and help a girl change her tire, not that she thanked me. At least, I have some time left to stop in and see you. You make the most amazing food on the planet. I need more of your mouthwatering pie, but we can't stay."

"No problem. Let me pack you up a pie to take with you."

"That sounds perfect." He glances over at me. His eyes narrow as he checks me out.

"Well, it's my pleasure, and Dynamo is welcome anytime."

He puts a hand over his heart. "What about me?"

Marge giggles. "You too."

It's weird seeing Marge blush, but I understand. The man is an irresistible force of nature.

The expression on Marge's face sobers. "Are you settling in okay?"

"For now, yes. And thank you." He takes a bill out of his front pocket and places it in Marge's tip jar. "Your diner is the highlight of my day." His steely gaze takes another passing sweep of the diner, lingering on me with no more interest than he gives the empty tables and chairs.

I sit up straighter, with rising indignation. How dare he ignore me. Is he doing it on purpose?

I'm not going to say anything, because he's looking for a reaction, and there is no way I'll give him the satisfaction of knowing he got under my skin.

It doesn't matter whether he acknowledges me or not.

Except heat rises in my cheeks and my heart hammers in my chest. My fingers tingle with an odd electricity zooming along my nerves. I resist the urge to run my fingers through my hair, combing out the tangles. If I do that, it'll look like I'm trying to grab his attention.

My lips are dry and I lick them before I can stop myself. That draws his eye for a split second, but that's all. He doesn't show any outward sign of interest.

No man deserves to be that good looking, or act that confident. He's the stranger, not me. Yet he acts as if he owns everything in that room. I really should look away. The scar running across his face says he's dangerous, but damn if that doesn't make me want to know him more.

His attention shifts from my lips back to my eyes, then he flinches and turns away.

"Come on, 'Mo. We have places to be." He walks out of the diner, powerful muscles bunching beneath the worn denim of his jeans. "Thanks for the dog treat, Marge. Until next time."

SEVEN

Dax

IN MY LINE OF WORK, EMOTIONS ARE LIABILITIES. PART OF MY training in special ops was learning how to control myself in every situation and override the emotions which weaken a man and destroy a team.

With the girl, I fail that task miserably.

There was no reason to wait for her by the side of the road. I told myself I was simply being protective, making sure she didn't need my help.

But that was a lie.

There was no reason to follow her into Bear Creek. I told myself I gave up on my trail run and would simply head to Crowbar ranch, calling it a day.

That was a lie as well.

When she pulls into a parking space across from the diner, I should drive past and leave her behind. I don't. I park and debate my next move.

Marge and her love of dogs gives me the perfect pretense to cross paths with the girl again. I take the opportunity and promptly blow it the moment I walk inside.

Something comes over me, an arrogance or foolish pride. Whatever it is, I crash and burn. I expect her to notice me, and thank me for helping her out. What I get instead is a cold shoulder.

Is she testing me?

It's almost as if she's angry with me, which isn't fair, because she was very clear about being able to help herself. I practically had to beg to do anything at all.

Too independent. That's her problem. Not mine.

Freely offered help shouldn't be perceived as an insult, but rather the favor it's meant to be.

Women are beyond confusing.

Not my fault if she wants to complicate shit.

I walk in with every intention of striking up a conversation, but at the cold reception she gives me, it's all I can do to ask Marge to give Dynamo a treat and not look like a complete fool.

Who the hell walks into a diner begging for a bone?

An idiot, that's who, and I drive off cursing the complete fool I made of myself. Perhaps it's good riddance to leave the girl behind. She cost me most of my day.

I didn't get in my run and that pisses me off. Working with cattle is good, hard work, but it doesn't lead to the mental and physical exhaustion pushing my endurance normally brings.

Not that the day is a complete loss.

I decide to head down toward Peace Springs and finally stop in on my friend. It's probably best to do that before Caleb finds out I'm in town.

Less than half an hour later, I pull up outside Rowdy Range. As I understand things, Caleb grew up around these parts and took over management of a relatively modest cattle operation after he was medically discharged from the Marines.

Dynamo hops out of the truck and sniffs at all the interesting smells. I go to the front door, knock, but nobody answers. Not that I expect anyone to be home this time of day.

"Come on 'Mo. Let's find Killshot."

A Marine scout sniper, Caleb was recruited into Delta Force precisely because of his lethal skill with his weapon. His nickname fits him perfectly, and yet still doesn't fully encapsulate the lethality Killshot brings to a mission.

I cup my hands over my mouth and call out.

Nothing.

Dynamo and I search the barn, but find no one working inside.

A modest operation doesn't mean Rowdy Range is small and there should be a few ranch hands around. It takes me half an hour before I track Caleb down, and I manage to get in some of the run I was craving as we search.

We find Caleb in one of the far pastures behind the barn. I jog toward the big man wrestling a fence at the far end of the field.

"Yo' Killshot!" I stop and spread my arms out wide. With his eagle eyes Caleb knows who I am.

"Dax?" Caleb shades his eyes and stares.

Unlike most men, I never earned a cool nickname during my time in the service. Or maybe, Dax was my nickname?

My father burdened a small boy with a name that never fit, and he refused to allow me to shorten Alexander to a more reasonable Alex.

I hated the pretentious name growing up—Alexander Kingston—and finally shed it in basic training when one of the female recruits mentioned Dax was short for Alexander.

She wound up with Bunny, a name she hated and I was given Dax. I didn't believe her about Dax being short for Alexander, but that's all it took.

The name stuck and was original enough to stick beyond basic training.

"Dax Kingston?" Caleb puts down the fence puller. "What the hell are you doing here?"

Now, that's a loaded question, and I'm not sure how to begin answering it.

As I near him, I note the eyepatch over Killshot's eye. It reminds me about the one thing we share. We're damaged goods.

"Just came to say hi." I came for something else, a sense of camaraderie I miss.

Caleb understands what it means to be one of the few privileged enough to serve in special ops. We don't share a service, but we fought and bled by each other's side. That's enough to form a lifetime bond.

"What the fuck did you do to your face?" Caleb drops his hand and gives me a long hard look. Then my expression softens and my brows draw together. "I take it you're out?"

I look down and kick at a rock. "Yeah. Got the big old thanks for your service, now leave."

"I feel ya'." Caleb wipes at the sweat on his brow. "So, are you just passing through? You could've called. We've got a spare bed if you need it for the night."

We.

After leaving the Marines, Caleb found his way home and got hitched to his high school sweetheart. Some people are lucky in love.

"Thanks, but I'm working at Crowbar ranch. I've got a place there, at least for the time being."

"Really? Whatcha doing there?"

"Helping Studer during calving season. He needed an extra hand and I needed work."

Caleb snorts. "You don't need the work."

I give Caleb a squint. We never talked much about our pasts and I'm pretty sure I never mentioned much about my family. Caleb doesn't seem to notice the hitch in my step and rolls on through the break in conversation.

"I could use a spare hand, too. Wish I knew you were looking for work. Didn't know you knew anything about cattle."

That answers that question and I breathe out a sigh of relief. I'm not ashamed of my family's wealth, or the reputation we've built within the industry, but I don't like to advertise it either. My issues are personal and have more to do with living out from beneath my father's shadow than anything else.

"I grew up in Texas man. We're born in the saddle."

Caleb laughs at that one. "I suppose that's true."

"I knew you grew up in a small town in Montana, but I didn't know you were here until someone mentioned your name. I wanted to come by and see how things are going."

"We're busy as fuck."

"I could always help out."

"I appreciate it. I really do, but there's no way in hell I'd poach a worker off Tom Studer. That man is solid."

"I get it."

"You settling down out here?"

I glance at the broken fence Caleb is trying to mend. "I'm actually just passing through. You know how it is, needed to get my head screwed on straight before I can figure out the rest."

"I see you picked up an ugly assed scar."

"That and more." I feel at the puckered skin on my face and hold back a grimace. I don't like being reminded about the disfigurement, but then Caleb lost an eye. The man understands.

Caleb points to Dynamo. "Nice dog."

"Smart dog. He's got herding flowing in his veins. I'm training him at Studer's ranch, but it feels more like he's waiting for me to catch up with him."

"Shit, I know what you mean. Cate has this Newfoundland…"

"Big black bear of a dog?"

"You've seen Bear?"

"I saw a massive bear-sized monstrosity of a dog at Marge's. Shit, if I'd known that was your girl, I would've introduced myself."

"How about we do one better. Come over for dinner."

"I'd love to, but like you said, it's crazy busy. Maybe next week?"

"Sounds good. I'll invite my friend Drake. He was in the community. Green Beret, if you can forgive him for that."

I laugh. Sibling rivalry between the services never gets old.

"We'll figure something out." Caleb arches an eyebrow. "While you're just standing there…"

I glance at the fence. "Yeah, you know you're doing that all wrong, right?"

"You got a better way?"

I push up my sleeves. "You Delta boys think you know it all. Now stand aside and let a real man show you how it's done."

"Zoomie."

"Gomer."

"Air Farce!"

"Jarhead!"

"At least we're not grunts."

"Oh, don't let Drake hear you say that." Caleb twists the wire I tighten, securing it in place. That's the problem with cattle. Normally, they stay away from the fences and the barbs which cut into their flesh, but sometimes, especially when spooked, they run right through them.

We joke back and forth as I help Caleb mend the fence. I show Caleb a few tricks I picked up over the years. Sometimes, brute force isn't the answer.

"You lost any cattle through this breech?" The sun is dipping toward the horizon. As it's my day off, I don't mind lending a hand.

"Yeah, but my men are on it. This fence opens into Drake's pasture. Our cattle are co-mingling right now, but they'll bring mine back."

"How big is his ranch?"

"A few thousand head." Caleb gives a respectful nod. "He's got the biggest operation out here. I think it might even be the biggest in the state." He jabs me in the ribs. "You may want to go easy on the grunt and cannon fodder jokes, my Zoomie friend."

"I look forward to talking to him. Never got to support the Green Berets."

"Have you given thought to what you're going to do once you sort things out in your head?"

I never mention PTSD, but there's no need. Caleb understands.

"Not really."

"Peace Springs could use a good paramedic."

As a part of my training as a Para Jumper, I hold a national certification as a paramedic. If I want, I can go anywhere in the country and settle down. Every town, city, and major metropolis needs paramedics.

But therein lies the problem.

My skin itches when it comes to thinking about settling down. My roots are in Texas. My blood flows in that land. There will come a day when I have to face my father's judgmental eyes and commit to the future I was born into.

But not today.

Today, I can work until sweat drenches my shirt and the sun sets below the horizon.

Studer gives me quarters at the ranch. He has a small one bedroom apartment in a building out back with a few other guys. We spend our days working, too busy with the cattle to trade life stories. Nights we spend apart. Not that I'm looking to make friends.

Bear Creek is nothing more than a layover as far as I'm concerned.

We finish up mending the fences and head back as dusk sweeps through the sky.

"Damn, but this really is big sky country."

Texas has skies which stretch to the horizon, but in this, Montana has bigger, badder, and much more impressive sunsets. The entire sky fills with sheets of liquid fire, bright golds which deepen to the burnt umber and dark crimson reds.

By the time we make it back to the house, curtains of the deepest purple usher in the blackness of night. The first stars pierce the night sky and a chill settles in the air.

I shake Caleb's hand, refusing to come inside to share a beer.

"You sure you won't stay?"

"It's getting late, and I have to be up before the ass crack of dawn."

"Don't I know it." Caleb pulls off his sweat soaked shirt and tosses in on the floor. "Don't be a stranger, and I'm telling Cate you'll be here for dinner next Friday. Are you helping Tom out with the fair this weekend?"

"I think so."

"Maybe we can have you over sooner. Tom won't mind."

"I'll think about it."

"Do that. Don't make a liar out of me, and I want you to meet Cate."

"I'd love to meet her." I rub the back of my neck. "Although, I think I kind of already did."

"You mean at the diner?"

"Yeah. She may not appreciate you inviting me over."

"Why's that?"

I relay my trip to the mountains, coming across the girl with the flat tire, and the awkward exchange in the diner.

"Oh, now that's going to be fun. I wonder who it was?" Caleb rubs his jaw. "She knows everyone in town. You get a name?"

It doesn't escape my notice that Caleb doesn't mention he knows everyone in town as well. Bear Creek is a very small town. He probably knows the girl too. For a moment, I think about digging for information, but Caleb is too smart. The last thing I need is the entire town talking about the stranger with the scar who has eyes for a girl.

I shrug. "We didn't exactly hit it off."

EIGHT

Dani

HEAT RISES ALONG THE BACK OF MY NECK AND I GRIP MY FISTS SO tight that my nails bite into the palms of my hands.

The nerve!

I finally have a name for the infuriating stranger. Dax called me ungrateful? Chastised *me* for not thanking *him*?

What the hell? The cocky bastard left me to fend for myself.

He should apologize to *me* and beg *my* forgiveness for being such an ass.

And really? What did he do? Loosen a few nuts?

Given enough time, I would've figured it out. Granted, I might still be on the side of the road, but I could've hiked until I reached a pocket of cell service. My dad would've come to my rescue...eventually.

The age of chivalry truly is dead, or maybe I simply have the worst luck with men. Dax should've done the heavy lifting and finished the job.

Maybe he left because I didn't gush over his physique enough? Men can be such vain pricks, needing validation for the simple act of breathing.

Although, he does know how to wear a pair of jeans, and I wouldn't mind seeing all that brawn beneath his shirt.

My frustrated snort in the diner amuses Cate to no end. The moment Dax walks out, Cate practically rolls on the floor. Even Bear stands up, shaking his coat and throwing slobber on the floor. Marge offers no support, even after I explain why Dax is the absolute worst asshole on the planet. The twinkle in Marge's eyes has me biting back several colorful phrases.

Well, Dax can kiss my ass if he's going to be like that.

Although, to be fair, Dax isn't the worst asshole in the country. Scott holds that honor.

"What do you think is so funny?" I prop my hands on my hips and turn my anger toward Marge.

"Oh, honey, you're too close to see it."

"What the hell does that mean?"

Marge exchanges a look with Cate, which sends Cate into a fit of giggles.

"He's pretty hot," my best friend says. "I think you're going to have problems with that one."

"That's what I've been saying. He's an arrogant asshole."

"Uh-huh." Cate exchanges a look with Marge, but whatever those two are thinking, I don't want to hear it.

After Cate picks herself up off the floor, and Marge finishes with her secretive looks, I excuse myself and head home.

With the sun setting, my father will worry if I don't make it home soon. I may not have called Cate, but I texted my father when I left

Pullman. It's one of his most stringent rules.

Text when I leave.

Text when I arrive.

By the time I drive down the last section of road before the ranch, I'm still fuming over Dax's intentional snub. I turn off the main road and onto the unpaved drive. Gravel crunches beneath the tires and a cloud of dirt lifts into the air behind me.

True to everything I know about my dad, he waits on the porch, rocking in his favorite chair. Blue smoke from his cigar curls around his head. He slowly rises from the chair, and I can imagine the sound of his boots scuffing the hard planking as he plants himself at the top of the stairs to welcome his daughter home.

A strong man, the years are beginning to wear on my father. We lost my mother a few years ago, and he lives on the family land alone, except for the few men who help him run the ranch.

They stay in a series of outbuildings and aren't necessarily welcome inside the main house. My father keeps the house exactly as my mother left it, wrapping himself in the love her memories bring. I understand not wanting others intruding on that solace.

I feel bad leaving my father all alone, but my education is important to him. He chases my dreams nearly as hard as I do, encouraging me every step of the way. He hooks his thumbs in his belt loops and puffs on his cigar. Leaving my bags in the Jeep, I run up the stairs and into my father's arms.

"Daddy! I miss you." I wrap my arms around his lean torso and place my cheek against his broad chest.

The rich scent of cigar smoke permeates his shirt, and I can't help but take a deep breath. Cigar and pipe smoke will always remind me of home. I tried to get him to quit, but smoking is the one vice he clings to with stalwart determination to never change. He politely told me he will smoke until the day he dies. We agreed to disagree, and I silently enjoy the richness of my daddy's unique smell.

"Danielle, I missed you too." He whispers my full name and envelopes me in his strong arms. "It's good to have you home, luv."

We stand there for a moment and simply absorb each other's love.

Finally, he pulls away and looks deep into my eyes. "I thought Scott was coming?" He glances at my hand. "Seems there's something missing."

My friend, Cate, doesn't hold the market on intuition. My father has always been able to read my thoughts, or sort out a situation with one look. It made it challenging growing up because I was never able to get away with anything. My father always ferreted out the truth.

My eyes prick with tears, but I'm not willing to waste any emotional energy on Scott.

"I broke things off."

"What?" He takes a step back, more of a stagger, and shock deepens the lines of his face. "Why? You're engaged."

"Was engaged. Past tense." I swallow against the lump in my throat.

"What happened?"

"Scott slept with Beth."

My father's eyes widen and he pulls me into a hug. "I don't believe it. He loves you."

"It was the night of the Spring Formal." A tear slips out. "I blew all my exams afterward. I couldn't focus."

"I'm certain you did well on your tests. You're a smart girl."

"You're not upset?"

"Why would I be upset? Give it some time. I'm sure the two of you can figure things out."

There's something in his expression. Anger and rage, but also something much more concerning. My father's smile falters, as if the bottom dropped out of his world.

Or maybe, I imagine the reaction, transferring my residual emotions onto my father's expressions. Whatever it is, my father recovers quickly. A soft smile turns up from the grim press of his lips.

"I don't think there will be any *figuring it out.* Not after what he did."

"There has to be more to the story, Danielle. You've got some time apart. Once you see each other again, and have a minute to talk, maybe things will be different. You're a smart girl who thinks everything through. You'll figure this out too."

My father likes Scott and already accepted him into the family. He doesn't understand there will be no going back. Scott and I are a thing of the past, but I'm not going to argue with him. He'll have to process the disappointment on his own, just like I will.

I grip my father's shirt and give a light tug. "It's good to see you."

My father and Scott get along well, and Scott asked my father for his blessing before presenting me with that ring. It must be a disappointment to know the son he thought he was getting turns out to be the biggest douchebag in the world. And I know the two of them talked about the ranch and what the future might bring. Scott is supposed to take over operations while my father moves into retirement.

Calling off the engagement affects my father as well.

I don't know what will happen now. There are no sons to hand the ranch down to, and I have a career as a veterinarian to pursue.

He grips my shoulders and bends down until he can look me in the eye. "He's lucky he's not here. If he were, I'd cut his balls off."

"Daddy!"

"I would. Either that or use him for target practice." He wipes at my tears. "We'll make do and he's going to be sorry when you take over the world."

"I'm not taking over the world."

"With all your girl power? You're definitely taking over."

I laugh beneath his praise. He's always been my number one fan.

"We'll see."

"You can do anything you want, Danielle, and he's a fool for cheating on you. But, don't make the mistake of closing off your heart." My father releases me and straightens to his full, towering height. "Now, let's get inside and put some food in your belly. Are you hungry? Or did you stop at Marge's for pie?"

"Pie and ice cream. Cate was there."

"Ah, well, I'm surprised you came home at all. I'm sure you two wanted to catch up." He takes the steps off the porch gently and retrieves my bags from the back seat of the Jeep.

"I knew you'd be waiting and I didn't want you to worry."

"You could've called." He takes the steps back up in slow motion, not because of age, my father is a man who never hurries. His idea of rushing is to bend his head downward and saunter with a bit more swagger. That's just the kind of man he is, born with a calm disposition and a steady outlook.

"I know, but I wanted to see you." I hold the door for him.

He wraps an arm around my shoulders and ushers me inside. The rest of the evening we spend talking about my school, my plans for next year, and the clerkship opportunities which might be available.

He wants me to take my clerkships in Montana, as close to home as possible, but I don't want to limit myself if I don't have to. He doesn't push, or force his wishes on me, but continues with his steady support and confidence that his little girl can do anything.

I ask how calving season is going, knowing the ranch tends to struggle this time of year and he asks about my drive home.

"I got a flat."

He arches a brow. "You did?"

"Yes. A guy stopped to help."

"Really?" He leans forward and places his elbow on his knee. "You were safe?"

"I was safe."

"You can never tell. Did you have your gun?"

"Yes. I had it."

"You didn't try changing it yourself?"

I explain about the problem with the lug nuts and the less than stellar man who helped, then abandoned me to finish the job.

"Well, that's strange, but it's hard to find good men. Seems like he helped as you needed it." Somehow, my father knows there's more to the story. He'll never ask, and will never accuse me of having a smart mouth, but it's implied in the way he rolls the cigar between his fingers and in the long, steady look he levels my direction. "I assume you managed to change the tire since you're sitting here?"

"I did, no thanks to him."

My father shrugs. "Sometimes helping someone can be problematic. I wouldn't read too much into it."

"I can't believe you're taking his side."

"Not taking any sides. Just saying I know my daughter."

"What's that supposed to mean?"

"I didn't raise you to be a damsel in distress."

"Doesn't mean I don't need help from time to time."

"Now, that's probably the wisest thing you've said all night. Sometimes, it can be hard to let others help. This isn't the first time you've had this problem."

That comment has me flopping back on the couch with exasperation. I've always been strong willed. My father raised me to be independent and I let everyone know I can take care of myself. Sometimes, that comes at a price.

"I don't want to talk about that anymore. Tell me about the ranch. Have you found any help?"

"Well, I hired on a good man. He knows a lot about cattle and is a Godsend."

"Good. I'm glad to hear it." My father needs someone who is a real asset to help out this time of year.

We talk until he starts to yawn. Still early in the evening, I shoo him to bed, knowing he'll be up before dawn. In the echoing silence, I clean the dishes and head to the back porch to read before going to bed.

A chill hangs in the air, but it's not too cold that I'm uncomfortable. Unseasonably warm for spring, I enjoy the stillness of the night air and stare up at the sky looking for shooting stars. As I daydream about my future, the stars put on a show.

Then I see it.

The ruddy glow of a fire on one of the distant hills. Someone is out in the back pasture. Flames flicker in the night, but don't spread. It has to be a campfire. Nobody should be out there, and I consider waking my father to check it out.

But it's late, and I don't want to bother him. I will, however, investigate first light. If there's a drifter camping out on our land, he needs to be dealt with, sooner or later, and one way or the other.

Eventually, the warmth of my bed calls to me and I snuggle beneath the thick blankets, drifting off into a sleep filled with dreams of a man who knows how to fill out a pair worn blue jeans.

NINE

Dani

BRIGHT LIGHT WAKES ME THE NEXT DAY, SHINING THROUGH A GAP IN my curtains. I stretch and pull on a faded pair of jeans, my boots, a tee-shirt, and a light jacket for riding. A quick peek inside my father's bedroom confirms he's already gone.

I fix a light breakfast, then head out to the barn. My horse, Honey, whinnies when she sniffs at my approach, and we spend a few minutes reconnecting before I take her out of the stall and saddle the mare.

With my backpack full of supplies, I plan on a day roaming the ranch. I don't know how often my father gets Honey out for a ride, and decide to spend the day with my horse while the weather holds. This time of year, blue skies and fair weather are transient things to be enjoyed, and I have deep thoughts to sort out. Top of that list is how to deal with school, and avoid Scott, while I finish out the semester.

Honey enjoys the freedom of being out of the barn and I give the horse the lead, nudging gently with my knees to guide her toward the back pasture and the hill where I saw the campfire last night.

Honey picks her way across the field, walking and cantering, flicking her tail, and enjoying a little taste of freedom. Eventually, we make it to where I think the fire should be, and sure enough, some asshole built a ring of rocks. The charred remains of a fire blacken the ground inside.

A quick check reveals a man-sized depression in the low grass, the tracks of a single horse, and more concerning, the deep impressions of one of my father's cattle, probably a bull by the depth of the tracks.

I need to speak with my father, because there's no reason for anyone to be traveling across our lands. Cattle thievery, in general, is a thing of the past, but there are still stories of the occasional rancher who has to deal with unscrupulous men.

I follow the tracks. This close to the mountains, our ranch is more a series of rolling hills than flat plains. A river runs through the land, forming steep bluffs with sharp drop offs to the river below.

That river begins just above Bear Creek, after which our town is named. Bear Creek winds its way down from town, joining with other tributaries, and grows wider and calmer as it enters our land. Crystal clear with snow runoff from the mountains, I spent most summers swimming in the icy waters. It's one of the few ways to escape the sweltering summer heat.

This time of year, however, the water in the river is barely above freezing, which is why the sound of splashing draws me up short.

I veer away from the path the interloper took and crest the rise of a bluff which overlooks the river. The tracks of the man's horse, and the bull, veer to the south, working down to the river.

Alone, I'm no match to meet a man head on, but I can take a look from the safety of the bluff, not to mention I have a gun. I dismount Honey and tie the mare to a low hanging branch of one of the few trees just out of sight. I walk the rest of the way up to the bluff, crouching low so as not to reveal my position.

My eyes widen when the naked man in the water stands to his full height. Broad shoulders ripple with muscles and taper down to muscular back and tight ass. Holy sculpted masterpiece.

My jaw drops.

He faces away from me, running his hands down his body, then suddenly his entire body goes still. He cocks his head, listening, then returns to washing himself. His clothes are stretched out on a boulder sticking out of the water within arm's reach of him. They dry in the sun and I spy toiletry items on top of the clothes.

The muscles of his back flex as he scrubs at his hair and he runs his hands across the front of his chest, moving them in circles. My mouth goes dry thinking about all the hard angles and ridges of muscles on the front of his torso.

His movements are slow, sensual, and full of masculine perfection, completely entrancing, and he moves as though he's aware of everything and anyone. Only, he doesn't seem to be aware of me peeking over the edge of the bluff.

I want him to turn around and silently send out a plea for just that, as if the universe will grant such a wish.

A rich lather covers his head, trickles down the broad expanse of his back, and washes away in the slow flowing waters. The firm globes of his ass flex, and I prop up on my elbows to stare at the perfection of his lean, muscular body.

That's when I notice the scars across his shoulders and along his back. There are so many and they're relatively new. Pink, puckered skin draws tight into angry lines. From the tip of his shoulder to the crack of his ass, the entire expanse of his back is littered with horrific scars; a testament to a horrendous injury in his recent past.

I can't help but gasp.

He immediately erupts into action, leaping toward the boulder and pulling a rifle out from beneath the stack of clothes. When he spins around, I slam flat against the ground and pray he didn't catch me spying, but the rifle is already rising and pointing directly where I hide.

"It's not polite to stare." The deep, rumbly bass of his voice penetrates the distance. "I know you're up there. Might as well show yourself."

It can't be. This man is my stranger.

I peek down. He lifts his chin, eyes glinting with steel. He squints against the early morning light and there's no denying the truth.

That is Dax.

How did he know I was up on the bluff? I was absolutely quiet and there's no way he could have heard that tiny gasp.

Water streams down his nakedness and when he straightens, his body moves with a sinuous glide of power and lethal intent. The water reveals more than it hides beneath his waist. His chin lifts, bringing the intensity of his gaze to pierce the distance between us. Although half a river and a forty-foot bluff separates us, I feel as if he could leap the distance in a heartbeat.

Reason says I need to inch back, run for my horse, and gallop the hell away, but I find myself pushing off the ground as I reveal my position. A few steps, and I stand at the edge of the forty-foot cliff. I'm ready to lock myself in a battle of wills with the most confusing man I've ever run across.

Standing at the edge of the bluff, I glance down at the near side of the river. Under a copse of trees, his horse and a bull munch at the tender spring grass, while a dog curls up on the ground. That dog lifts its nose and sniffs the air.

Silence descends between us, echoing in the beating of my heart and thundering in the ragged pull of my breathing. The wind whistles across the rolling hills, but it's the stillness between us that makes me suck in my breath.

"You don't belong here." I finally manage to get the words out, and fumble with the gun in the holster at my hip.

"Says who?"

"Says me." I aim the gun at him. "I don't know who the hell you think you are, but this is private land. I'll call the Sheriff."

"Go away, little girl." His husky drawl whispers across my skin, lifting the fine hairs of my arms.

"You go away. You don't belong here." I widen my stance and lift my gun. "I have a gun."

"So I see." His eyes pinch. "Do you know how to use it?"

"I'm a decent shot."

"Somehow, I'm not impressed." He lifts the barrel of his rifle. "I, on the other hand, am an expert marksman. How about you put that pistol down before you hurt yourself?"

"You arrogant prick."

"Wow, such manners, although I'm not surprised. You seem to have difficulty with gratitude."

"Me?"

"Yes, little girl. You. The one pointing a pistol at me while I'm naked and defenseless."

"You don't look very defenseless and you're pointing a rifle at me."

"Only because you're trying to sneak up on me."

"I'm not sneaking up on anyone." I point to the bull. "I'm tracking down a cattle thief."

His face breaks into a cheeky grin. "Is that what you think?"

"Proof's in the pudding. That bull belongs to my father. If you don't leave right now—"

"You'll what?" He keeps the barrel of his rifle pointed at my chest.

Unlike my pistol, which grows heavier with each second, he holds his without any sign of fatigue.

I have a mind to shoot over his head and prove him wrong about my aim, but my father would tan my hide. The only time I'm allowed to shoot at a person is with the intent to kill and only if my life is threatened. If my father finds out I let anger get the better of me, I won't walk for a week.

"I haven't done anything wrong." He takes a step forward. The water lapping at his waist dips, and the V-shaped ridges of muscles over his hips angle down, dragging my gaze with them

Dax continues out of the water; every step occurs in slow motion. He doesn't rush and keeps his gaze locked on me, through the sight of his rifle. The confidence in his stride keeps my mouth gaping and my pulse pounding. He slowly rises out of the water revealing every glorious, and erect, inch of his tight and toned, body.

My breath hitches and I lower the pistol. He makes no attempt to hide his erection, or any other part of his body.

He walks away from the clothes spread out on the boulder in the middle of the river and slowly lifts the barrel of the rifle to adjust for his new position.

"Like I said, little girl, it's not polite to stare. Do you like what you see? Because you really should be paying attention to me and not my cock." His expression slips.

I gulp, eyes fixated on the perfection of his body and the prominent evidence of his arousal. Is that because of me? Or is it simply the way men are?

Although, that water is cold. His cock should be a shriveled thing. So why is it…

His husky drawl is all the more potent due to the thick Texas twang layered on top. He continues to walk out of the river, closing the distance, and moves with such stealth I can barely hear the tread of his feet on the soil. The man moves like death, a lethal powerhouse of deadly force I should run away from. But, my feet are rooted in one spot and there's no way I can turn my back on...*that.*

Thankfully, I have the protection of the bluff. Steep walls keep him down by the river and me safely forty-feet up an impassible cliff, although I have a sinking feeling that won't stop him. I tighten my grip on my pistol.

"Stop calling me little girl. I'm a grown woman."

"A woman has no business tracking down a stranger alone."

Shit. I didn't think of that.

"I'm not alone."

"And I'm not stupid, although I'm beginning to question your sanity. Do you know how dangerous it is sneaking up on a man? How do you know I'm not alone?"

"You are."

"But did you know that?"

"I followed your tracks. One horse. One bull. One man."

He cocks his head. "You may not be as stupid as you look."

"Name calling? Your manners suck."

"As I remember things, your manners could use a little work."

"I have a gun. And what do you mean *my* manners. You left me. Was I supposed to thank you for that? What happened to chivalry?"

"I have a rifle, which is bigger than your tiny pistol, and I know how to use mine. I'm not yet convinced you know how to use yours."

His sexy tone dresses me down, and damn if that doesn't do strange things to my insides.

"You'd be dead if that's what I wanted, or worse," he says. "As for your flat tire? You were pretty clear about not needing any of my help. Now, turn around and go home. You don't want me coming up there."

I'm about to give him a piece of my mind, when my left foot shifts half a step back and my torso twists; turning around just as he commanded. Heat fills my cheeks and I ball my fingers into fists. No way is he telling me what to do.

I jerk back around, and take a step forward, ready to show him a thing or two, when suddenly the ground beneath my foot gives way. I try to jump back, but gravity has something else in mind. The gun drops out of my hand as I fall, arms windmilling over my head.

TEN

Dax

LIFE ON THE RANGE BRINGS BACK-BREAKING WORK, LONG DAYS, AND shorter nights. It's a hard life, but provides the solitude I need to get my head back in the game.

I spend most of my days mending fences, hauling hay, minding the herd, and sweating like a pig. Rather than spend my nights in the barracks provided by Studer for his men, I prefer sleeping beneath the stars as far from humanity as I can get.

There's something about living on the land which soothes my soul. It brings me back to my roots as a child, and feeds the devastation of my soul. A war hero who's forgotten and unappreciated, I need this connection to my roots without the overbearing judgement my father would heap upon me.

It isn't a Texas sky, but the setting sun paints the same devastating canvas beneath Montana's skies. The stars look the same as I stretch out in my sleeping bag and stare into eternity.

Everything is great.

Day by day, my anxiety fades and peace settles in. Where the simple act of breathing once required work, the open air, earthy scent of grass beneath my feet, and the ever-present chirping of insects in the springtime breeze loosens the tightness strangling my every thought.

This place nourishes me.

The one day off I had since coming to work for Studer, found me heading out of town where I found a girl, followed a girl, and haven't been able to get her out of my mind since.

Now she found me.

Is this the universe's idea of a joke?

My heart speeds up with her sexy spitfire and defiant glare. Our banter back and forth lights a fire in my gut and sends electricity licking along my cock, awakening my body and the urges within. The chilly waters hold no sway over the heat surging in my groin. In seconds, I'm tense, aroused, and incredibly erect.

The more she yells, the harder my dick becomes.

Then, in a second, everything changes.

Time slows down.

One moment, the girl stands forty feet above me. The next second, the ground gives way beneath her feet.

She tumbles over the edge. Her arms windmill as she falls.

She drops and I run.

I fling my rifle to the side and it bounces on the dirt. Gravel bites into my bare feet as I sprint to the base of the bluff.

A fall from that height can break a leg, or worse. It can snap her neck, killing her instantly.

Propelled into action, I don't think about anything other than saving the girl, but I won't be able to get to her in time.

She screeches, arms flailing, and slides down the steep incline. That might be what saves her life, because she's able to grab at a root and stop her fall. A few inches below her feet, a rocky outcropping forms a tiny ledge. It can't be more than a few inches wide, barely large enough for her to stand on.

If I can get her to that ledge, I might save her life. Already, the gears in my head churn, measuring the time it'll take to either climb up to her, or race to the top of the bluff and rappel down. A quick scan, and I decide there's no safe way to climb up. The cliff is more dirt than rock. There's nothing I trust to bear my weight.

Dangling overhead, she kicks in the air as she clings to a precarious handhold. Sand, dirt, and gravel falls down, dropping on my head as I race to the foot of the cliff.

"Hang on!"

I whip my head back and forth, up and down, assessing the situation in the span of a breath. Cracks form in the dirt around the root. It won't hold for long, especially with the way she flails.

She faces outward from the cliff, and keeps trying to flip herself around. I understand why. I'd feel more comfortable facing the cliff too, but there's nothing there for her to cling to stronger than that root. She'll be more stable with her back to the cliff, facing out.

All she's doing is making things worse. I need to calm her down.

"Stop kicking!" I bark the command and glance up into her wide, terrified eyes.

Each time she tries to twist around, she dislodges more dirt. I have only seconds.

"Listen to me." I use my command voice to break through her terror. "You're going to have to let go."

"Let go? Are you crazy?"

"There's a small ledge a few inches below your feet. I'm going to get you through this, but I need you to do exactly as I say." I wait for her thrashing to ease.

Her breaths huff overhead, followed by a whimper. When her movements don't still, I take a step back.

"Look at me."

She closes her eyes, and I blow out a breath, trying not to let my frustration show.

"What's your name?" Maybe distraction will help.

Her lower lip trembles.

"Tell me your name."

Her eyes pinch, but she opens them, slanting her gaze down to look at me.

I'm directly below her, which makes it difficult for her to see me. It's a risk to take a few steps back, but I need to calm her down if my plan has any chance of working.

I debate how far to step back, weighing in the speed of my reactions in case she suddenly lets go, or the root breaks free.

I soften my voice, making it as soothing as possible. "What's your name, hun?"

"Dani." Her attention shifts down to me, lands on my face, then slips down the expanse of my naked body.

I swallow and hold back a snide grin. How funny is this? Me talking to a girl, butt naked, as she dangles overhead, clinging to a root?

"Listen, Dani..." I love the way her name sounds on my lips. It's short, crisp, but has a feminine fluidity to it. "First off, I've got you. You're going to be okay. Do you understand?"

She shakes her head, a fractional nod that says she isn't convinced but has no other choice than to put her life in the hands of a stranger.

Fortunately, situations like this are exactly what I spent a lifetime training for, and I'm the best of the best. I'll get her out of this alive, but she needs to trust me.

"Dani, this is what we're going to do."

She twists again. Her overwhelming urge for self preservation has her seeking the safety of the dirt behind her. The only problem is it's exactly the wrong thing to do.

"Do. Not. Move." I lift my voice, injecting power into each word. She'll listen. There's simply no other alternative.

She stills beneath my command, and damn if that doesn't send the wrong message to my dick which has no part in this exchange. But I can't help it. The power which comes from her surrender to my commands lights up every nerve in my body. I shake my head and focus on Dani.

"Now, listen. We don't have much time." I don't want to tell her about the cracks forming in the dirt around the root, but they widen each time she moves.

"What do you want me to do?"

Finally!

I want to shout with victory. She's finally going to listen instead of argue.

"Okay, there's a ledge beneath your feet. You need to trust me on this. We need to get you on that ledge, but you have to let go of the root."

"Let go?" Her lids draw back with terror. "If I let go, I'll fall."

"If you fall, I'll catch you. But, you're not going to fall."

"You promise?"

There's no other option. I need her to get to that tiny ledge, then pray she doesn't fall while I race to the top of the bluff.

"I promise, Dani. Now listen. I need you to be very still, put your back to the dirt behind you. There's a very slight slant, and we're going to take advantage of that. When I say so, I want you to release your hand." That will shift her body an inch lower. If she points her toes, she'll find the ledge.

"Now?"

"In a second. I want to talk you through this. You can't see what I see, so you need to trust me. There's a small ledge just below your feet. You're going to release your hand and that will lower you down just a bit, but you're not going to be able to feel the ledge. You're going to have to drop that last inch, but if you're very still, and listen to exactly what I say, it's going to be okay."

She gives another tight nod and pinches her eyes shut. Then she suddenly jerks.

"My grip's slipping!"

"You've got this, Dani. You're stronger than you know. I want you to take in a deep breath and let it out. Tighten your grip on that root."

She follows my instructions.

"Next, I'm going to tell you to place your free hand as far out to the side as possible."

Her entire body shifts down and to the right. The toe of her boot taps the edge of the tiny ledge.

"That's it. Do you feel that?"

"I do."

"I'm not going to lie. It's small, barely enough room for your foot. But if you keep your back to the dirt and your hand out to the side, you can slip down to that ledge. Keep. Your. Back. Flat." I enunciate my words. "And keep your head pressed back. I don't want you looking down. I'm your eyes. Understand?"

If she looks, her head will tilt forward. Her shoulders will follow. That'll be all it takes to overcome the delicate balance needed to keep her on that ledge.

"You ready?"

I don't have much time. Her grip is slipping, and with only one hand holding her up, she'll fatigue quickly.

"Yes."

"Okay. Eyes Closed. Head Back. Press your back to the dirt. Flex your feet. We want your heels on that ledge. If you're ready…"

Before I can finish, she lets go. As I expect, she doesn't drop, but rather friction between her and the rough dirt and rock has her sliding the final inch to the ledge. Her heels contact the rocky outcropping and her slide stops.

ELEVEN

Dax

"Good job, Dani." I use her name on purpose. Saying it over and over, I hope it'll keep her calm. "You're doing great. Now, this is going to be the hardest part, and where I need you to trust me the most. How do you feel? Steady? Do you feel like you're going to fall?"

She swallows and licks her lips. Her lids press tight together.

"I feel the ledge. It's solid."

"Good." I glance up and assess her position until I'm satisfied. "Keep both hands out to the side. That'll keep you steady. I need you to think about leaning back, pressing your head, your shoulders, your back, your butt, and your thighs back against the dirt. If it helps, keep your eyes closed."

She follows my commands.

"What now?"

"I'm coming to get you, but I need to get you from the top of the cliff. It's going to take me a minute." I need to put my clothes on before I do anything else. Butt naked, I'm not much help.

"Don't leave me."

"I'm not leaving you, but I have to step away from the bottom of the bluff. Have you ever rock climbed?"

"No."

"Okay, that's no problem. I've done this before. I'm trained in mountain rescue, but I need to get dressed…" Butt-assed naked is not the way to conduct a rescue. I clear my throat, glad she can't look at me. "I'm taking my horse to the top of the bluff. I'm going to rappel down to you and take you off that ledge. But I need you to stay calm. Don't move."

"I'm scared."

"You're doing great. I find it's easiest to keep my eyes closed and count my breaths." I back away from the base of the bluff, while I coach her through a breathing exercise.

All my clothes are on the boulder in the middle of the river. There's nothing to do but wade through the chilly waters and retrieve them. I waste precious seconds trying to shove wet legs into the denim, but finally manage to dress myself and put my boots on.

I keep talking to Dani the entire time, telling her what I'm doing as I try to keep her mind off the fact that if she breathes the wrong way, she'll fall.

"I'm going to the top of the bluff, now. You won't be able to hear me until I get to the top, but I'm here, and you're safe."

"Okay." Her legs shake and her fingers claw at the dirt.

I don't have much time before a sudden movement, dizziness, or disorientation tips her over the edge and sends her tumbling to her death.

For a moment, I think about having her open her eyes. She'll be able to balance better with her eyes open, but that ledge is tiny. The toes of her boots stick over the sliver of rock. If she looks down, the rest of her body will follow.

I leap onto Cassidy, my chestnut stallion, and kick the horse into a gallop. Cassidy's hooves dig into the ground, kicking up heavy clods of dirt, as I launch around the backside of the hill.

Dynamo follows, running beside the horse, keeping a perfect heel. Studer's wayward bull keeps to the meager shade under the small tree and chews its cud.

I ride all out, keeping low in the saddle, until Cassidy crests the rise of the hill.

Nothing.

There's nothing to anchor a belay line for the rope. I leap off Cassidy and put my hands on my hips. Cassidy is new to me, but has years of experience beneath other men's reins.

Dani's horse stands a little down the hill. I turn to my horse and grip its long face, staring deep into its eyes.

"Can I trust you?"

I hate placing my faith in an animal I don't fully trust, but I need something to anchor the end of my line. I hoped for a tree or a heavy boulder, but there's nothing nearby.

I grab a rope off Cassidy's saddle and count out the length. With a quick slice, I cut a ten-foot section to fashion a Swiss Seat, which will form my harness. I measure again, making certain I have enough rope to reach all the way to the bottom of the bluff and made a second cut, leaving me with three pieces of rope. With ten feet to spare, I tie one end of the rope to the pommel of Cassidy's saddle.

"How are you doing?" I call down to Dani.

"I'm good." Her voice cracks.

"I'm coming."

Many climbers spend hundreds of dollars on expensive harnesses and other gear, but the truth is all a person needs to safely rappel are two pieces of rope. A small, ten-foot piece to form the climbing harness, and the rappel rope itself. Easy to make, a Swiss seat is safe, surprisingly comfortable, and takes less than a few minutes to tie.

I take the short rope, fold it in half and place it around my waist. The two free ends go between my legs and to my back. I feed them around the rope at my waist, tightening as I go. A little adjustment of the family jewels, and I make sure there will be no painful pinching. I squat down three times, pulling the ropes out and away from me to tighten them. This ensures a comfortable fit. I bring the ends around to my hip, tie off a square knot, then add half hitches to either side.

The Swiss Seat doesn't work without a carabiner, but I always carry one on my belt loop. Incredibly useful devices, I use them for everything. I clip the carabiner in place and then check my work.

The entire time, I tell Dani what I'm doing, soothing her with my words, and remind her she isn't alone.

Satisfied with my work, I go to my horse. "All you have to do buddy is stand still."

At just over a thousand pounds, Cassidy can easily bear the weight of me and Dani on the line. I just worry about the horse pulling against the weight.

I toss the line over the edge of the bluff, making sure not to hit Dani. She flinches as it strikes the dirt, wobbling ever so slightly on the ledge.

"Head back!" I bark. "Don't move."

"Dynamo, you stay with Cassidy." My dog plops down, placing his snout on his front paws. His brows tent and his ears lift. Dynamo cocks his head as I back up to the cliff. I hook into the line and tell Cassidy, one more time, to stay put.

Slowly, I put more weight on the line, eyeing the horse, but Cassidy doesn't budge. Satisfied, I slowly lean out and back, placing my faith in a horse.

Dani hovers just a few feet down.

"I'm at the top and coming down. You may feel some rock come loose. I'm to your left. Just don't move."

"Okay." Her fingers clutch at the bare earth, digging tiny trenches into the soil.

I lean all the way back, placing my weight on the line and planting my feet on the edge of the cliff. Normally, I would bounce down. It's the quickest way to the bottom, but that would place excess stress on Cassidy as my weight comes off the line then back on.

I walk myself down to Dani, breathing easier as I draw alongside. Now, for the tricky part. I need to get her on the line.

"I'm here, hun. Just a little more and we'll get you down. How are you doing?"

Her eyes pinch tight. "Can I open my eyes?"

I hover beside her. "In a second. What I'm going to do is straddle you." I'll place my body over hers, caging her between me and the rock.

I kick out from the wall, spread my boots wide and swing into position over top of my girl. When I do, she lets out a deep sob, and almost breaks down completely. I only have one hand free, the other holds the rope and secures me in place. I reach up and wipe a tear from her cheek.

"Open your eyes, Dani. You're safe. I have you."

We're close. Terribly close. The floral scent of her shampoo mingles with her fear-sweat. It feels like a slice of heaven.

My large frame completely brackets her small form, obliterating nearly all the space between us. I think she'll break down completely, but my girl has a head on her shoulders.

She cracks open one eye, but her hands don't move. She presses them hard against the dirt, along with her head, her shoulders, her back, her hips and every incredible inch of the rest of her body.

The heaving of her chest brings her perky tits into view and it's all I can do not to focus on them. I force myself to look into the depths of her eyes, losing a part of my soul in the process.

"Wrap your arms around my neck. I'm going to tie you to me."

Tying a makeshift harness around her proves difficult. Normally, I'd tie a victim to my back, but this situation requires creativity. It's not ideal, but I'll make it work.

When her arms wrap around my neck, electricity shoots down my spine, jolting my cock with a rush of pleasure.

Unexpected, it's not entirely unwelcome. I keep a check on my belay line with one hand while I wrap the last length of rope around her waist, over her shoulders, then around my waist. Not a Swiss Seat, the contraption acts more like a harness.

Her pillowy soft breasts press against my chest and her terrified breaths flutter across my neck. She buries her face against my neck and the wetness of her tears does something strange to me. They free a constricting band from around my chest I didn't realize was there. It comes as a surprise, making me fumble with the last knot.

With the strange pulsing sensations zinging down my spine, and her wet tears doing strange things to my chest, I groan as I ask her to do the unthinkable.

All I have to do is get her down thirty-some-odd feet.

"Dani, wrap your legs around my waist. I've got you. You're tied to me. You're safe."

She gives a tight nod, but doesn't move her legs. I shift away from the wall and cup my hand around the back of her thigh. Her entire body tenses, but I give firm pressure, and slowly force her to lift her leg and wrap it around my hip. She balances on the heel of her other foot. Every instinct in her head probably screams not to lift that leg, but it's the only way to get us down.

"Grip my neck."

I keep my tone calm and smooth, and try to imagine she's nothing other than any of the hundreds I've helped in combat. The truth is she's nothing like those battle hardened soldiers. She's soft, fragile, and wonderfully female.

Remaining professional takes an act of God, but I manage. I put my hand on the small of her back, run it down the curve of her ass, to where the crease between her butt cheek and thigh would be. Leaning out, I lift her leg, and bear the entirety of her weight.

"Close your eyes, luv."

Not willing to waste another second, and unsure about Cassidy's strength to bear both our weights, I push outward with my legs and let the length of the line run through the leather of my glove.

We swing out, and Dani's entire body squeezes around mine. I bite back a groan as the heat of her pussy presses against my belly. This is not the time to get hard, but blood rushes to my dick anyway. It doesn't care about the life and death situation.

We drop about ten feet before slowly swinging back. On my own, I would drop much further, but I have her and Cassidy to consider. I plant my legs on the wall, absorb our momentum, and kick out again. After another two bounces, I land on the ground at the base of the bluff.

"We're down." I release the rope and wrap my hand around the small of her back. Dani doesn't climb down, but squeezes her legs around me instead. Her entire body shudders with her cries.

Not knowing what to do, I simply hold her in my arms.

TWELVE

Dani

___

SOME LIFE EXPERIENCES SHAPE THE SOUL. CLINGING TO THE SIDE OF a cliff is one of those moments I will never forget. It changes me forever.

Dax holds me, soothing me with low murmurs I don't understand. I don't need to, because the deep rumble of his voice tunnels into my soul, wrapping itself around my heart, and releasing something inside.

I cling to him, knowing I shouldn't, but I can't help myself. I don't want to let go.

He doesn't force me down, and seems to carry my weight with ease. A whistle pierces the air, blowing past my ear. It makes me jump. The high pitched tone warbles and is answered by a bark from the top of the bluff.

I squeeze my eyes shut and take in a breath. Clutching Dax, I snuggle against his chest, seeking reassurance in the steady beat of his heart and the deep draw of his breath.

Bigger up close, his size makes me feel tiny and delicate, nearly inconsequential as he walks us away from the cliff. There's a tugging at my side, then the rasping draw of rope as he unravels the makeshift harness which ties me to him.

More barking sounds, along with the distinct clomping of hooves, draw my attention to the bluff.

"Good boy, 'Mo," he calls out. "You even brought Cassidy down."

I crack open one eye and lift my head. A dog and a horse trot down the sloping hill to the edge of the river. A long length of rope trails behind the horse, and I give a start.

Dax lifts a hand up to the horse, calling it in, which leaves only one arm wrapped under my butt. He continues to hold me, as if my weight means nothing, and walks up to the horse.

As he does, he slides the rope tying me to him off my shoulders and drags it from around my waist. The rope drops to the ground, and I suddenly find myself lifted into the air as he sets me in the saddle.

"Grab hold."

He waits until I steady myself, then tugs and pulls at more rope tied around his waist and legs. After he frees himself, he wanders off a short distance and retrieves his rifle and my pistol which fell to the base of the bluff.

Securing his rifle in the holster attached to his saddle, he vaults onto the back of the stallion, and settles in behind me on the saddle.

The earthy scent of loam and springtime grass fills my senses. A light wind tickles my cheek. Billowy clouds fill the sky and a strong arm wraps around my waist.

I tense as Dax kicks the horse's flanks and makes a series of clicks and clucks with his mouth. The horse responds, turning around, and angles toward the bull standing beneath the shade of a tree.

Dax leans forward and the entire expanse of his broad chest presses against my back. I can't help the sharp inhale of breath and hope he doesn't notice. He works at a knot on the pommel, loosening the long length of rope.

It's dangerous to tie a rope like that and let it drag on the ground. A horse can step on it, get tangled, and foul its legs.

Dax's actions are fluid movements as if he and the horse are one. It takes a lot of skill to move like that. Before I realize what's happening, he coils the rope and ties it to the side of the saddle.

"Let's get you home." The warmth of his breath whispers against my cheek and I can't help but shiver. He yanks the rope keeping the bull in place and ties it to the saddle.

With another series of clicks and the slightest pressure on the reins, the horse heads up the rise. The bull ambles behind us, huffing as we go. Dax makes a beeline to where I left Honey and in another fluid series of movements, soon has Honey's reins secured as well.

"I can ride." I shift in front of him, intensely aware of his proximity.

"I know, but you're shaking like a leaf. Try not to argue with me about this."

"But…"

"Stop. I'm not putting you in the saddle. Not after what you went through. Just sit back, relax, and take a moment to breathe. You're alive."

"I know. It's just…"

"Breathe. There's no reason to talk." The bar of his arm tightens around my waist and he tugs me tight, soft and snug against his chest.

What I should do is argue. Although, it seems as if he isn't going to have any of that. There's no reason for me not to ride Honey, except tremors shake my body and my nerves feel like they're crawling under my skin. My legs aren't any better. They feel like jelly.

He's right. I'll probably fall off if I try to ride Honey.

I grip his arm to steady myself and lean back against him. Tilting my head back, I take in a deep breath and blow it out as slow as possible.

The stallion twitches its powerful muscles between my legs as he heads home. Come summer, the trails will be dusty, but this early in the morning, springtime dew clings to the grass and keeps the dirt where it belongs.

The ride out took me well over an hour, at this pace it'll take nearly half again as long to get home. That's an hour and a half of Dax's arm wrapped around my waist. His chest pressed against my back. His muscular legs wrapped around mine, and I don't want to think about the hard length pressing against the crack of my ass.

I take another breath and blow it out.

"How are you feeling?" His thick Texas drawl shivers across my skin, making me squirm with a restlessness I don't understand.

"Better." I swallow against a thickness in my throat. "I didn't say thank you."

"You just did." His arm flexes, tugging me tight.

"I should have said something sooner. Thank you for saving my life."

He presses his lips against my ear. "You're welcome."

One touch. The whispered heat of his words is like a lancing shard of heat, spearing me in the heart. He sniffs my hair and pulls the long lengths over my shoulder.

"I'm not sure how you're used to getting a fella's attention, but how about we knock flat tires, guns, and dangling from cliffs from the list?" The low rumble of his laughter rolls down my spine bringing devastating warmth with it. "I'm really not that hard to get. A bite of pie and some coffee is usually enough to pique my interest."

My spine stiffens at that comment.

"Why you…"

"Ah, there's your spirit. I thought you were going into shock there for a minute."

I dig my fingernails into his wrist. "You don't have to squeeze me to death."

"I know." Instead of releasing me, he gives a sharp yank, until there is nothing separating my ass from what lies between his legs. "Maybe I like it?"

"Maybe I don't."

"Do you find me repulsive?" He stiffens and pulls back.

"Why would you say that?"

"I didn't. You did."

"I didn't say I found you repulsive." Where is that coming from?

The man is drop dead gorgeous, every woman's fantasy, and he's a bonafide hero. He saved my life, and from one of his comments earlier, it seems he saves lives for a living.

"You said you don't like me holding you."

I love everything about him holding me, not that I'll admit it out loud.

Leaning back, I fold into the contours of his body. Hard and lean, that proves difficult, but I'm not wasting this opportunity as we cover the rolling terrain of the ranch on horseback.

I don't ride with anyone. Like ever. From the moment I wore boots, I've been on the back of a pony, then a horse. My father took me trail riding when I was a little girl. That was the only time I shared a saddle with another person.

My father encouraged my independence, nurtured it, and always told me I can do anything I want to do.

"I take it this is your land?"

I give a tight nod.

"For the record, I'm not stealing the bull."

"Excuse me?"

"The bull. You know, the two-thousand pounds of choice beef plodding along behind us. He doesn't seemed particularly thrilled about it either. I think he's interested in checking out the heifers in the next pasture."

In the excitement of falling over a cliff, I forgot about what brought me out this way.

"What are you doing with the bull? And was that you last night?"

"You'll have to be more specific? I did a lot of things last night." A deep rumble of laughter vibrates through his chest.

"I'm not sure I want to know *everything* you did last night, but I'm talking about the campfire. Was that you?"

"Hard to know for sure."

"What does that mean?"

"I don't know where you were last night. You could've seen any campfire."

"I was sitting on the back porch of my house, looking out at the pasture."

"Ah, yeah, that was me."

"What were you doing out there?"

"Minding the campfire."

His short, clipped answers infuriate me, but I keep my anger in check because I'm one-hundred percent certain he's having fun at my expense. I hold in an exasperated sigh and bite my lower lip while I count to three.

"Why did you build the fire last night?"

"You may not know this, but it gets chilly outside at night."

"I know it gets chilly." I suppress a growl. Bastard is having fun with me. "You know what I mean."

"I actually have no idea what you mean. I'm not a mind reader."

"You're teasing me and being purposefully obtuse."

"Obtuse? That's a big word."

"You need me to use small words?"

He laughs. This time it's a full belly laugh, a deep rumble which takes over his entire being, and is easily the sexiest thing I've ever felt.

And I do feel it.

I feel it in the sweep of his breath against my cheeks, in the tightening of my hand over his wrist, and in the flutter sweeping through my belly.

"No need for small words. I can handle the big ones too. How about you?"

"How about you answer my question?"

"Is this an interrogation? Because I have to warn you, I'm trained to resist interrogation."

I jab my elbow back, poking him in the ribs. "Is that so?"

"Actually, it is."

"Well, I don't care about that."

"But you do care about why I was out last night?"

And the truth is, I not only care, but it fascinates me. In fact, everything about him intrigues me, but how to dig for information when he won't answer the simplest questions? Time to be direct.

"If you weren't stealing the bull, what are you doing with it?"

While I can't see him, I feel the twitch of his smile.

"He broke through the fence last night and wandered through my campsite. When I woke and saw the tracks, I went to fetch him and bring him back."

"Bring him back where? Do you work for my dad?" I'm not normally this dense, and realize how stupid I sound. Why can't I think straight?

"Looks like you're starting to connect the dots. Dax, at your service."

"You're returning the bull?"

"Ring a ding, another point for stating the obvious."

I cross my arms over my chest, unwilling to give him the satisfaction of stating the very obvious. Somewhere along the way, I managed to misplace about fifty IQ points.

Come on Dani, you're not this dumb.

"If you work for my dad, then you have a bunk in the bunk house. Why would you sleep outside?"

"I don't like people."

"You don't?"

"Well, I might be convinced to like certain people, but I like my space."

"Camping outside?"

"If the weather's not too bad. We had good weather last night."

"How many nights have you slept outside?"

"You have a lot of questions."

"I'm curious."

"About me?"

I don't want to admit it, but it's the simple truth. There's something about Dax I find insanely attractive. Granted, it probably has something to do with him saving my life, but from the first moment we met, I haven't been able to get him out of my head.

"Yes."

"Well, I've answered quite a few of your questions. How about we turn things around?"

"How's that?"

"My turn to ask the questions and you have to answer with the truth."

The flutter in my belly turns into an all out tidal wave of anxiety.

The truth? How damaging can that be?

"Okay?" My voice wavers with uncertainty.

"My first question is simple. Will you give me an honest answer?"

His deep voice whispers across my skin and skates across my nerves, lifting the fine hairs of my arms. The words tunnel deep, landing squarely in the core of my being. Hypnotic and intoxicating, I find myself answering before I fully think about the consequences.

"Yes."

He presses his lips against the side of my neck. "Remember, you promised."

"Okay." I swallow against the lump in my throat as something fundamental shifts between us.

"When you imagine yourself in your lover's arms, what do you want to feel?"

THIRTEEN

Dani

DAX'S QUESTION DROPS THE BOTTOM OUT OF MY WORLD, LEAVING ME suspended over an impossibility.

What kind of question is that anyway?

When you imagine yourself in your lover's arms, what do you want to feel?

The question rattles around in my head, and I can't help but wonder.

What do I want to feel?

It isn't a question I'm prepared to answer because I have no idea what I want to feel.

Love?

Certainly that, but that seems too easy.

Content?

Not quite right either. It lacks passion.

Maybe that's what I want to feel? A soul consuming passion which fills me with the knowledge I'm loved. Maybe that's it? What I know for sure is I don't want the devastation Scott's kind of love brings.

Given an impossibility, what would love *feel* like?

I have no idea.

Love hurts.

It cuts deep, leaving impossible scars.

Scott was supposed to be my forever, but his love hurt. It cut. It slashed at my heart, leaving nothing but destruction in its wake. And he didn't care. He blamed *me* for catching him in the act. Like it's *my* fault I'm not worthy of love.

I believe him.

Or did.

The truth is I hate Scott. I hate the vulnerability he exposed in me. I hated opening myself to his pain.

A silence hangs in the air between me and Dax.

Not Scott. But rather the man who saved my life.

The silence between Dax and me vibrates and shudders, growing into something indescribable with each halting breath. Dax's question causes a hitch in my thoughts. It wavers between each beat of my heart. Truth grows there, fades, then returns. Undeniable, I can't ignore the pulse of what exists within this moment.

There's no way to explain the stream of consciousness swirling in my head.

But I know.

Truth cuts deep.

I'm not enough. I'll never be enough. Not with Scott.

But Dax?

Is he the lover in his question? Is he bold enough to assume that he is?

There's no question about it. He is. How did I go from dangling over a cliff to accepting him as my lover?

I don't know, except for feeling the truth in the lightness of my stomach, the racing of my heart, and in the warmth spreading outward from my chest.

He represents something I don't understand. A force which pushes and pulls and can't be denied. Somehow, he worked his way inside, making me feel things I shouldn't.

"Um, that's a bit personal." I hitch up a shoulder and roll my neck, realizing how tense and sore my body feels after my ordeal. Or maybe that's the excuse I use to convince myself Dax means nothing.

"The best questions always are." The bar of his arm cages my body against his, leaving little room to squirm. He isn't letting me escape the intrusiveness of his mind-blowing question.

When did I descend into this fresh hell?

But his question remains at the forefront of my thoughts.

What do I want?

How should love feel?

It certainly doesn't feel like the sting of betrayal from a man cheating with his first cousin. My stomach churns with revulsion as images of Scott and Beth twisting in the sheets runs through my mind.

That's the short and dirty answer, and I should go with that.

Love sucks.

Love lies.

Love betrays the innocent.

It hurts.

However, I sense Dax won't accept something that trite.

He'll drag the truth from me until I confess my deepest thoughts. Not that I'll let him win this round, but there's something about him, some quality, that makes me think I can trust him with the most intimate truths. That alone has me considering the insane question, but pride and indignation rear their ugly heads.

"Why would you care?" I snap, biting out the words.

"I didn't think you'd answer." The teasing in his tone vanishes beneath disappointment.

"That's one hell of a question from a man I barely know."

"Is that so?"

"Yeah." I twitch and he releases the pressure around my waist.

I lean forward, and immediately regret the loss of the soothing warmth of his chest pressing against my back. Now that I force distance between us, I can't exactly *lean back*. That would be weird. But now, I'm stuck perched forward in the saddle, which puts me in a very uncomfortable position.

"I'd say you know more about me than you're willing to admit." There's a sense of victory in his words, but also extreme restraint.

I understand neither.

I have no retort to fling back at him, which brings an awkward silence to the ride.

And he's wrong.

I know nothing about him.

Except, he's the kind of man who stops to help a woman stranded beside the road. He loves to test me. That had to be what he was doing in the diner. Or, maybe he's just checking up on me, making sure I'm safe?

He lives free, thinking nothing of spending the night outside. He chases down bulls, bringing them safely home. He put his life at risk rescuing me. He holds me with a possessiveness I don't understand. And, most concerning, he delves deep into my head, settling himself in the cracks where he's beginning to take root. From the first moment we met, I haven't been able to get him out of my head.

The muscles of my lower back tighten with the awkwardness of my position, making me regret pulling away from him. He lets his arm drop, switching the reins to that hand. He runs his hand through his short, close-cropped hair. It reminds me of the military, which kind of fits the stranger behind me, and the questions I asked before.

Polite to a fault, he carries himself with unwavering confidence, but if he is military, what is he doing on my father's ranch?

I take a leap of faith. "Why did you leave the military?"

"Are you asking more questions?" He gives a low chuckle. "That's not how things work."

It's exactly how I want *things* to work, because his question is insane, dangerous to answer, and I need the protection deflecting his question brings.

"It's a simple question," I say with a huff. "I don't mean to offend."

"Oh, I'm not offended, just amused…and curious."

"What does that mean?" I put my hands on the pommel and stretch out the tight muscles of my back.

My entire body aches. Every muscle is deeply fatigued. Maybe all the adrenaline zinging around my body is beginning to fade, leaving me with the lingering after effects of my near fatal fall?

"I'm waiting to see how hard you try to avoid my question." His smile is something I can't see, but feel deep inside.

"It's a bogus question and incredibly personal."

"It's honest. We breached the personal barrier when you wrapped your legs around my waist and buried your sweet face against my chest."

"You put *my* legs around *your* waist. You make it sound like I hopped your bones. When you say it like that it makes me sound like…"

"Like what?" His tone turns gruff. "The next words out of your mouth had better not be *cheap*, because that's the last thing I'm thinking. Stop being a pain in the ass, you can't ride all the way back perched like that." He grabs at my waist and yanks me back against him. "Accept the inevitable."

What the hell does that mean? I want to ask, but hold my thoughts.

No.

What I want is to issue a challenge, and I fight the urge. There's something about Dax which raises my hackles. Do people have hackles? I don't know, and I most certainly don't understand my reaction. It makes me curious and insanely cautious. Dax doesn't follow any of the rules, and that leaves me to flounder. The last thing I need is uncertainty. Maybe it's time to take back some degree of control?

Maybe?

But, what if I allow the impossible? What if I allow him a chance to take control?

"I can ride my own horse." I want to lean against Dax, but I stiffen and jerk away.

"Not happening." He gives a low growl and wraps his large frame around mine. Normally, something like that would have me running for the hills, but with Dax it somehow feels right. That makes no sense, except that it does.

What does that mean?

"I'm feeling better." I try to argue.

Perhaps, I test his resolve? Maybe I want to see what he'll do? Who knows? Who cares?

"Good, now stop squirming." His Texas drawl tunnels along my nerves, setting fire to my body, and sending my thoughts into a tailspin. "Settle down. I'm not putting you on your horse."

"Let me go." In direct defiance of his wishes, I squirm.

"No."

"Why not?"

"Because I like the way you feel in my arms. I'm not ready to give that up and I'm not convinced you won't fall out of the saddle if I let you go. Relax. We're not that far." His tone turns snide. "I'm sure you can tolerate being close to me for just a little bit longer."

"That's not what I mean."

"Isn't it?"

He places his palm to my belly, splaying his fingers out wide. The edge of his thumb brushes against the swell of my breast. He moves the finger away, and I don't know why that bothers me as much as it does.

Nothing makes any sense.

"No. It's not."

Since he forces me back against him, I allow myself to relax, absorbing more of his comforting presence. As soon as we get back to the ranch, this ride will end. The fantasy, such as it is, will fizzle and dissolve.

The sad truth is, I don't want it to end.

His question turns over and over in my mind. The rolling of the stallion's gait rocks me back and forth, moving me against the pillar of Dax's body. The slow movement heightens my awareness of everything about him.

An energy pulses in the air between us. It crackles beneath my skin and skates along my nerves until it delves deep inside to my core. His presence fills every breath and surges in every beat of my heart.

The crackling sharpens, digs deeper, and travels lower where it forms a knot of sensation between my thighs. My jeans feel itchy and my body burns. Every sense heightens, and they all zero in on the man who holds me in his arms.

Behind me, Dax says nothing, letting the silence between us stretch and the aching need within me build until my throat feels like it's closing in on itself, letting my breaths stagger into my lungs.

Honey whinnies and the bull snorts. The stallion expands its rib cage as it draws in deep breaths. Overhead, the rolling clouds thicken with the promise of rain. Behind me, Dax breathes with a solid assurance everything is right in the world.

His resolute confidence makes me ask the impossible.

"If I answer your question, will you answer mine?"

"That's generally how things work."

I imagine his lips curving up in victory, but don't feel as if I lost this round.

I think hard about how I want love to feel like and how it failed me in the past. Then I take in a deep breath, close my eyes, and wrap my hand around his wrist.

"I want sleepless nights and conversations without end. I want passion, madness, and someone who will make my entire body shiver with one look from across a crowded room. I want someone who will pull me close and make me feel as if I not only belong, but am an indispensable part of them. I want them to see my flaws, embrace them, and show me how they're my greatest strengths. I want love without compromise. I want to face the storm and know I'm not alone. I don't want an ordinary love. I want the impossible."

I bare my soul, giving him everything in one breath. Then I sit still. My chest heaves. My heart pounds. Regret creeps into my thoughts.

What the hell have I done?

He says nothing, yet his thoughts are telegraphed in the movements of his body. In the tensing of his legs. In the way his breaths hitch. He tells me everything.

He splays his hand across my belly, keeping his touch modest and yet at the same time, incredibly sensual. Possessive. Protective.

Dax's chest swells with the deepness of his breath, then it's as if his entire body curves around mine, claiming me as his own.

He wraps his arms around me, sheltering me. The warmth of his breath whispers past my ear, sending a shiver down my spine and a tickle shooting up my neck.

I tilt my head back against his shoulder.

"That's..." He clears his throat. "That's not what I was expecting." He tugs on the reins and his horse ambles to a stop. "Who hurt you? Who took your heart and broke it?"

"I never said..." The pain of Scott's betrayal pinches at my chest. It's been less than a week. There's no reason I shouldn't grieve that loss, but I've yet to deal with my anger. "I never said that."

"You don't need to." He presses his lips to the corner of my ear. "Whoever he is, he's a fool. You deserve far better than someone who would dare to treat you that way."

I don't know about that. Perhaps I'm destined to be unlucky in love.

All the signs were there but I was too desperate to be in a relationship that I ignored the warning signs. Maybe that's a truth I need to accept? Until I learn to love myself, how can I expect someone else to love me too?

Dax gives a soft kick to his horse's flank, urging it back into a slow walk.

"Out of all the questions in the world..." I swallow against my indecision, but I need to know. "Why ask that?"

"Because it takes great strength to answer something that forces you to take a risk, and being honest with someone reveals your vulnerability. Thank you for that, by the way."

"Um, okay?"

"I mean it, Dani. From the moment our paths crossed, you've shown me nothing but strength. It's like we're locked in a battle of wills, but there's no reason for that. I was beginning to wonder if you were human, you just showed me you are."

"Human?" A grin spreads across my lips. He's back to teasing me.

"You aren't afraid to take on the world. I was beginning to think you were a tool, but now I know the truth."

"And what is that?" I ask.

"You're a lot like me."

"How so?"

"Because I believe the same thing. I want the storm and the power that rages between two people. But I'm not willing to share that passion and the madness with the rest of world. I want you all to myself. I've never found someone strong enough to give me what I need."

I purse my lips and blow out my breath. He wants *me?* Things just got a little too real, and I don't know whether to run or jump his bones.

What I understand is that we're close to home. I look across the field and spy my father waiting as he always does by the back porch. Arms crossed over his broad chest, his judgement and protectiveness radiate outward.

"Uh-oh." I grip the pommel.

"What?"

"My father."

"And?"

"How well do you know my dad?" I scoot forward and place distance between me and Dax.

He pulls me back to where I belong.

"I know him well enough."

I twist around, knowing it is a mistake as soon as I do.

Dax is too close.

Our lips are too close.

The heat of his breath is too hot.

"You have no idea what he can be like."

"I'm not worried about your father. Not when I have everything I want right here."

Dax closes the distance, leaving me in awe. The heat and hunger in his expression echoes within my thoughts. We barely know each other. Each time we've met, we've fought. And yet...

"Dax?"

He draws his thumb in a line from my ear, across my cheek, to circle around my lips. My breath catches as he gives a devastatingly slow smile. I can't look away, although I should, because he clearly means to steal a kiss I'm not prepared to give, but I have no intention of stopping him.

He cups my face and holds me still while he lowers his head in slow, agonizing degrees.

I have time to stop this. Maybe that's his intent? Forcing the choice on me? But my body is incapable of moving, not with the fire simmering in his eyes.

Even my lungs seem to have seized up, frozen between one breath and the next, as if the moment will stretch out forever if I hold my breath. My throat locks tight, leaving my heart to struggle in the overwhelming silence. Each beat pulses in my veins, and throbs in my lips, as if lighting a welcome beacon for him to come in, to take, to claim.

His mouth meets mine, the warmth of it stunning, and my entire being reels beneath the sensation. There's no avoiding this.

No pulling away.

Truthfully, I don't want to move out from under the gentle pressure of his mouth upon mine.

Heat spreads outward from my lips, fanning across my face, traveling down my neck, and descending further still.

I think that will be the end of it.

A chaste kiss after the harrowing ordeal of my rescue, but his tongue presses against the seam of my lips, demanding to be let in. And I oblige.

I open my mouth in sweet surrender. He sweeps in, claiming with bruising aggression, as he takes and plunders.

My gut tells me I shouldn't let a man I just met kiss me with this much passion. There are many things about it that are wrong. Most concerning is my recent separation from Scott.

There should be a mourning period before I allow myself to fall under another man's spell. Dax's tongue slides against mine, bringing a gasp to my lips. The way he holds me, gentle yet powerful, has to be one of the most intimate things I've ever experienced.

I crack an eye open and look across the field at the stony countenance of my father.

Arms locked over his chest, my father pivots and goes inside.

Is he getting his gun?

FOURTEEN

Dani

Dax leaves me in the horse barn and returns the bull to its pasture. While I remove the saddle from Honey's back, I brush the pads of my fingers over the puffiness of my lips. His taste lingers there, coiling deep into my soul.

A kiss from Scott never tasted that sweet, felt that overwhelming, or had the power to sweep me off my feet. In Dax's arms, beneath the press of his lips, something fundamental shifted within my heart. It's as if the steel bands encircling my heart spring loose, releasing all my pain.

Relieved of that burden, warmth pours in. Dax's essence rushes into the crevices and cracks of my broken heart, healing me from the inside out. Is such a thing even possible?

I never imagined a force of such aching beauty. Splaying my fingers over my chest, the slow *Lub-dub* of my heart beats with not only the knowledge it's true, but with a sense of becoming whole.

Honey whinnies as I lead her to her stall. I give her a few treats before securing the latch to the stall door, shutting Honey in for the night. When I turn around, a shadow falls across the ground.

"Danielle." My father steps into view, his tough features hidden by the bright light shining behind him.

"Hi." I smooth my hands on my jeans and step toward him. Straw crunches beneath my boots and dust motes dance in the sunbeams streaming through the cracks in the barn walls.

"Who is that you rode back with?"

A rhetorical question, he knows the answer, but I play his game.

"That's Dax."

"Why were you on his horse?" He takes a long look at me. His astute gaze travels from the crown of my head to the tips of my boots.

I can't help but shift beneath that gaze and gulp at the hard tone of his words. He makes me feel as if I did something wrong. I swallow against the lump forming in my throat and glance down at the straw littering the ground.

"He helped me."

"You don't need help riding, Danielle, and that's not an answer."

"Did I do something wrong?"

"That depends." He shoves his hands into his deep pockets and rocks back on his heels. His hard gaze holds me captive, and his stern expression hints at a lecture to come.

"Depends? What do you mean by that?"

"He's not for you."

"But—"

My father holds up a hand. "Dax won't be around for long. He's moving through and not someone you should get attached to."

"What does that mean?"

"A man like him isn't for you."

"Why would you say that?"

"I want you to be careful." He steps close and takes my hands in his. Running his thumbs over the backs of my hands, his voice lowers and turns serious. "I know things between you and Scott are difficult right now, but you have your future to think about."

"Things between Scott and I aren't difficult." I can't believe I have to explain this. "They're over. I thought you understood."

"I understand you're both dealing with a lot of stress, but you and Scott have history together and a future stretching out before you. He comes from a good, solid family, a family which can help ours."

"Help ours?" I pull my hands out of his. "What does that mean? Help us? Are we in some kind of trouble?" That doesn't make sense. My father's cattle operation is doing well.

Our land has been in the family for generations, and we've run cattle on it from day one. The land always turns a profit, but the shadows in my father's eyes say otherwise.

"Daddy, is there something I need to know?"

He sucks in a deep breath and spins around. Digging his fingers into the thickness of his hair, he paces up and down. "Nothing that needs to concern you, but don't throw your future away on someone you don't know."

"If you're talking about Dax, I think there's something real there." I clutch at my chest, feeling the warmth of Dax's kiss simmering inside. "I can't describe it, but it's not what I felt for Scott."

"Scott is a solid man."

"Who cheated on me." My hands curl into fists and heat rises to fill my cheeks. Why is he arguing with me?

"Who made a mistake." He won't meet my eyes. That's not like him. Shoving his hands into the back pockets of his jeans, he gives a slow look inside the barn. He examines everything, surveying the state of the barn without once looking at me.

Slow and steady, his tone urges me to consider the unthinkable.

"Do you want me to be unhappy?" I don't believe that's the case, but the Scott he welcomed as his future son-in-law isn't the man I know Scott to be. Scott might care for me, he may still, but he made a huge mistake.

It's unredeemable.

My father spent his entire life protecting me. Some would say overprotecting me, but his heart is in a good place. He wants only what's best. What does he know about Dax that I don't?

Not that it matters. Dax is ten times the man that Scott is.

I stamp my foot. "Scott cheated on me with his first cousin. How can you take his side?"

"I'm not taking his side, but I'm asking you to think about things, think about your future before you throw everything away. People make mistakes, just be careful you don't make a mistake that Scott won't be able to forgive. A spring break fling isn't proper, and it's not the way to get back at your fiancé. It could ruin everything."

"What do you mean ruin everything? There's nothing to ruin. Scott is out of the picture and that's that."

"I just want you to think about your future and the security Scott can promise you."

"He can promise me a lifetime of heartbreak never knowing if he's cheating on me. You can't want a man like that for me. Please, daddy, tell me that isn't so."

"Love isn't everything. He comes from a wealthy family. That's not something you should walk away from. Security like that is worth a little forgiveness. You're a smart girl. Think about it."

"I don't need Scott's money. Once I graduate and get my business up and running, money won't be a problem."

My father told me not to worry about the cost of my education. He always said he would handle it.

"Starting a business costs money."

"I can get a loan." I'll mortgage my future to see my dream become a reality.

"We already have loans." Shadows fall across his face as he glances at me. Yet again, he refuses to look me in the eye. That isn't like him and sends a shiver fluttering down my spine. A lightness settles in my belly when his features sag, telling a story I don't want to hear.

"Is something wrong?" He's keeping something from me.

"No honey…" He runs a shaky hand through the unkempt mop of his hair. "It's just your school is more than I thought. I needed to borrow against capitol for the ranch and those loans need to be paid back."

"You did what? I could have taken out loans. I can still take out loans. All I have to do is go to Student Aid…"

"I have the money, but it comes with obligations we can't back out of."

"I don't understand."

He breathes out a deep sigh and turns toward the door. "You shouldn't have to worry about this. I told you I'd take care of you, but what's done is done. We need to think about what happens next. Think about what Scott can do for you. What his family can do for us. He's not a bad man, just one who stumbled. All men make mistakes, but he'll be good to you in the end. I'll talk to him and explain."

"There's nothing to explain, daddy. I don't understand why you're pushing Scott on me. I like Dax."

"You need to leave Dax alone. He's a drifter; a wounded man. It's charity that I gave him work at all."

I sense greatness in Dax, not something broken. My father is wrong, and I'll show him how very wrong he is.

"I don't want to talk about this any more."

"All I'm asking is that you give it time. Don't do something you'll regret, at least not until I have a chance to sort things out."

I'm not sure what there is to sort out, but my father seems to think my future rests in his hands. That may have been true growing up, but I'm a year away from graduating. Finances tie me to my father, an unfortunate situation which shouldn't be a problem. There's something I'm missing, and I'll get to the bottom of it.

I brush past my father, jerking out of the way when he tries to grab my arm. I stomp outside and look around. Unfortunately, there's no sign of Dax.

Not wanting to appear needy, or have my father's troubled gaze follow me, I head into the house and call my good friend. There's a chance Cate knows something I do not.

"How's it going?" Cate's bubbly greeting brings a smile to my face, replacing the frown from the barn.

"It's been an interesting day."

"Really?" Cate's voice rises in pitch and I can practically see my friend leaning forward for something juicy.

"I met someone."

"Yes?"

"You remember that guy from the diner?"

"Flat tire guy? The one who left you on the side of the road? The one you couldn't stop drooling over at Marge's?"

"Okay, okay. That's enough, but yeah, that one."

"That guy really knows how to fill out a pair of jeans."

"Doesn't Caleb get mad when you check out other men?"

"Oh no, he knows where I sleep, but tell me about your guy. How interesting is interesting?"

"Well, I thought he was a cattle thief."

"You know he works for your dad?"

"Well, I do now." I explain about seeing the campfire last night and tracking him down.

"You saw him naked!" Cate gives a squeal through the phone loud enough that I pull the phone from my ear. "Is he as hot naked as I'm imagining?"

"Yeah." A flush heats my face. Dax is more than hot. He has one of those bodies women drool over.

"So, when you say naked…is that full frontal or just the ass cheeks?"

"Cate!"

"Well, a girl has to know. And did he cover up or let you look?"

"It wasn't exactly like that. He was in the water."

"Oh, you mean shrinkage."

"No. Not that." There was no shrinkage. "I pulled a gun on him."

"Holy shit! You don't mess around."

"Well, I thought he was stealing daddy's bull, and I was already kind of pissed at him. But I didn't get to see anything after I fell."

"Fell? What do you mean fell?"

I explain about the edge of the bluff giving way and Dax's rescue.

"You should have seen him, Cate. He's amazing."

"I just want to know if he put clothes on before or after he strapped you to his body?"

I blush fully now. That visual leads to only one thing, and I'm not ashamed to admit I'd like to get closer to Dax.

We talk about my ordeal. Cate screams and squeals as I tell her about all the juicy bits. I tell her about the kiss.

"I bet he's a good kisser." Cate sighs through the phone. "Men like ours usually are. Caleb knows him. Did you know that?"

"No. How so?"

"He said they ran a few missions while they were on active duty. He's medically discharged like Caleb and was a Para Jumper, special ops and medical. You two will be perfect together."

"Really?" I sit on the edge of my bed and cross my legs. "Tell me. I know nothing about him."

"How about you bring him over for dinner? Then we can grill him together and it won't seem so obvious you're digging for information. Caleb said he invited Dax over, but Dax can't come until next Friday. You think you can get him over here this weekend?"

"I'd love to, but I bet my dad is keeping him busy, and honestly I think he's going to try and keep us apart. He really wasn't happy when he saw us riding back together."

"Why's that?"

I explain about the very odd conversation with my father.

"What about the Spring Fair? It's going on this weekend. We can get together. The men can do their cattle thing while we hang out. Then we can tag team and interrogate Dax."

"Interrogate?"

"Sounds more fun than *ask questions.* Besides, he's one of those special ops guys. I'm going to ask Caleb tonight what he knows."

"Do that, then tell me everything." I glance out my bedroom window and watch my father walk toward the house. Head bowed, he's deep in thought.

"Look, daddy is coming in for supper. You talk to Caleb and I'll work on tomorrow."

"Gotcha. Let me know how it goes."

"I will." Fortunately, my father has to go to the Spring Fair. It's where all the deals are made for the coming year. He won't miss it, but that's okay. All I have to do is make sure Dax goes with him.

FIFTEEN

Dax

I RETURN STUDER'S BULL TO ITS PASTURE. THE ORDEAL WITH DANI took most of my morning, putting me hours behind in my work. I head back into the sweltering heat and join the herd, loving every minute of the backbreaking work. Dynamo lives up to his name as he buzzes around the herd, nipping at their legs and using his short *yippy* bark to make them go where he wants.

We work well as a pair. I identify a *heavy* and use my horse to separate it from the herd. This goes against the cow's instinct which is to seek protection with others. Dynamo keys in on the chosen cow, snapping at the legs of the others to move them away.

Together, we separate the *heavy*, corralling her into the near pasture closest to the calving barn. Cows drop their calves in the fields, but if a cow has difficulties with the birth, we'll guide her into the barn and help the process along.

I work with one of the other ranch hands, a silent man named Henry, who tends to keep to himself. A longtime resident of the local area, Henry doesn't trust newcomers and gave me a wide berth until I proved my worth. We work in relative peace now.

As the sun sinks below the horizon, the sweat on my back turns into a chill. Days are hot, but the nights can be brutally cold. Winter is not done with this land, but has yet to showcase one of its infamous Montana springtime blizzards. There will be frost on the ground come morning, but hopefully no snow.

With the day drawing to a close, I tip my hat to Henry saying goodnight. While Henry seeks the seclusion of the barracks, Dynamo and I head out to the fields where we'll spend another night under a star-filled sky.

Light streams out from the windows of the main house, leaving me to wonder which one looks into Dani's bedroom.

Something shifted within me when I held her in my arms, and I haven't been able to get her out of my mind, or my mouth. Her sweet taste lingers on my tongue. It's probably my imagination, but her essence seems to surround me all day.

That kiss.

From the moment I first saw her, a protectiveness rose within me. It's why I waited to make sure that flat got fixed, and how I found myself bumbling like an idiot in Marge's diner asking for a treat for Dynamo.

My teammates would have something to say about my behavior because I've never met a woman I couldn't walk away from. Hell, some women I ran away from, clingy women who thought one night meant we were soulmates forever.

I've always laughed at that—soulmates—but I'm not laughing now.

There's something wrong, a pain in my chest, a yawning emptiness which guts me from the inside out. Dani's absence makes me desperate to seek her out, if only to see what she might be doing. That kind of obsession makes zero sense, because I'm not that kind of man.

"Come 'Mo." I bark at Dynamo. It's time to head out for the night.

My preference for sleeping outside has more to do with avoiding the other ranch hands in the barracks than anything else. The itchy anxiety which grows inside of me eases with solitude. The noisy barracks don't give me that.

Dynamo cocks an ear and gives a low woof when I angle my horse back toward the main house instead of heading out toward the pasture.

What the hell am I thinking?

There's no way she'll let me in, and no way I'll jeopardize my job by fucking the boss's daughter. Although I sure as hell shoved my tongue deep into her mouth.

With a groan, I look at Dynamo. "You're right, 'Mo. That's trouble with a capitol T." I head away from the house and prepare to spend an achingly long night alone.

Rather than heading to my regular campsite, I turn toward the river. Something draws me there. Maybe it's because it reminds me of Dani. Her struggle on the face of that bluff was the catalyst which finally brought us together, turning angry strangers into cautious lovers.

Not that we're lovers.

Not yet.

I plan on changing that.

I hobble the horse and gather stones to make a ring for the campfire. With another night of clear skies ahead of me, I forgo setting up a shelter. There's something freeing about sleeping beneath a wide open sky. It soothes all the frayed edges of my mind after a long day around others.

Bedroll spread. Kindling lit. I sit beside the fire, feeding it fuel, and pull out a meager meal.

Twigs snap behind me.

I grab my gun and wheel around. When I see the intruder, my heart wants to explode. It can't be, but I can't deny what my eyes tell me is true.

She sought me out.

A cautious smile transforms her angelic face into something profoundly beautiful. The smile disappears beneath a hesitant grin. When her gaze softens the still air buzzes with a sparking of electricity. Or maybe that's just the beating of my heart?

"Is that how you greet all the girls?"

"Only those who sneak, or those who aren't invited." From the way her gaze falls, I kick myself for that last part. What a dick thing to say, but it slipped out without thought, a knee jerk reaction formed over a lifetime of pushing women away.

"And which camp do I fall in? The sneaking one? The uninvited one? Or both?"

I put my rifle away, setting it in the dirt, and stand to greet her.

One smile.

That's all it takes.

My heart belongs to her.

The air crackles and buzzes with an otherworldly energy flowing between us. The campfire casts her face in a canvas of shadows and ethereal flames. I question if I'm dreaming, because while I can't figure out why she would come to me, I hope it's what I fear; that she feels it too.

She wings up a brow and cocks a hand on her hip, jutting her leg forward. Her horse, Honey, stands behind her, snorting with each breath.

Dani doesn't run into my arms. She isn't that kind of girl. Instead, she sizes me up from a distance and taps a finger while waiting for my answer.

"You fall into the unbelievable kind. How did you know I would be here?"

Earlier, she tracked me from the remains of my campsite from the previous night, but there was no way for her to know to find me here.

A shrug lifts her shoulders. "It's kind of weird to be honest."

"How's that?"

"I couldn't sleep. My father said some things which have my head spinning and I needed to see you."

I point to my chest. "Me?"

"Does that surprise you?"

"It should." I take a step toward her. "But honestly it doesn't. I can't stop thinking about you. How are you feeling?"

"I should be shaken by my near-death experience." She tries to laugh it off, but it weighs heavily on her shoulders. Without missing a beat, she composes herself. "But it's the furthest thing from my mind."

"I'm that forgettable, huh?"

"Unforgettable actually." She clasps her hands together and twists her fingers. "That kiss..."

She lets the words trail out and casts her gaze down. Delicately, she nibbles on her lower lip, struggling to finish her sentence.

I shouldn't stand there and watch her struggle, but I can't help it. I'm dying to know what she'll say next. Not to mention, I find myself mute by her hot-as-fuck body and the effect it has on me.

My dick stands loud and proud, but that's expected when confronted by a beautiful woman. It's the more concerning changes occurring within me that bother me; things like the shifting of my heart, and the way she seems to be softening the hardened core I use to shelter my emotions from the world.

I want to tell her everything, to *share* everything. Never before have I wanted to do that with a woman.

Holy fuck, but she's done something to my mind. When she isn't confusing the hell out of me, with her spitfire attitude and righteous anger, she changes the very core of who I am.

How does a slip of a girl I barely know have that much power?

Explosive.

That's what it'll feel like to take her, but she's a mistake waiting to happen. I need to remind myself of that fact. There's no denying it, and I really should stop checking her out. Turning away, however, proves impossible.

"Well?" She glances up. "Aren't you going to invite me to share your fire?"

"That depends…"

"On?"

"What you were going to say about that kiss."

She glances at the stars, avoiding my question, but I can see her answer telegraphed in the tension of her body, the clasping of her hands, and by the way she nibbles at her lower lip.

"I wasn't going to say anything."

"Liar."

That grabs her attention. Fire sparks in her eyes and I feel the biting words at the tip of her tongue. Prepared for a tongue-lashing of epic proportions, she surprises me with a sigh and something much more profound.

A confession.

"I've never been kissed like that before. You touched my soul."

"I'd like to touch a whole lot more than your soul, but I think your father will have something to say if I take more than a kiss."

"I don't want to talk about my father. I want to talk about that kiss."

I spread my arms out wide. "I'm all ears."

Frustration builds within her, finding an outlet in the stomp of her foot. "Are you really going to make me ask?"

"Ask what?"

"Men are such pricks."

Her gaze takes in my face then dips to check out the broad expanse of my chest and my trim waist. The fire hides nothing from her view, and my dick demands equal attention. It tents my pants, growing harder by the second, and twitches when her eyes round in surprise. Her mouth gapes.

"I resemble that remark."

"I see."

I look down, unabashedly owning the erection. "What can I say? I've been hard for you from the moment I first saw you, and as far as that kiss…"

"Yes?"

I rub over my heart. "I don't know how, but you wedged yourself in here."

"Do you believe in love at first sight?"

I shake my head. "I don't."

"I don't either." She dips her head and stares at the dirt. "But if neither of us believes…" She lifts her face and regards me with glassy eyes. "How do you explain what's happening?"

I purse my lips, unwilling to deny what she says. I should laugh in her face and push her away. If she was any other woman, that's exactly what I would do. It would be a matter of self-preservation. However, the idea of pushing Dani away twists my guts.

She's already a part of me.

I gesture to the fire. "How about you join me by the fire and we can talk more about what neither of us believes."

Before the sun rises, Dani will be mine in every way. She already belongs to me. How that can be isn't something I understand, but things don't need to make sense to be true. When she hesitates, I can't help myself. I need to know how she'll respond.

"I'm going to ask you a question, and I want an honest answer."

"Okay." Hesitation fills her voice, but she extends her trust with the slightest nod. I know she'll answer whatever I ask, no matter how vulnerable it makes her.

"When you left your house tonight, where did you intend to spend the night?"

"In your arms." Without hesitation, she blurts her answer.

"Have a seat, Dani. We have a long night ahead of us."

She walks to the edge of the fire and stands beside me. At first, she holds her hands over the heat, but then she suddenly turns, wraps her arms around my waist, and presses her cheek against my chest. "Tell me you feel it too. Tell me I'm not crazy."

I wrap my arms around her, loving how her soft curves press against the hard planes of my body. I take in her scent and let it fill my lungs. In that moment, I know one thing.

I've found my forever.

"You're not crazy." I kiss the top of her head. "I hope this doesn't scare you, but I'm never letting you go."

SIXTEEN

Dax
___

I PULL DANI TO ME. GOD, BUT SHE SMELLS POSITIVELY SINFUL, BUT sweet as well. There's an innocence to her, which pulls at my protective instincts. I have to remind myself she's not one of the nameless one-and-done fucks I've used in the past to satisfy my physical needs.

This is a moment to savor.

Dani is a woman to appreciate, and God help me if I move too fast.

Heaven.

That's what she smells like, wildflowers and sunsets interlaced with cool breezes and long starry nights. I can hold her in my arms for an eternity and never get enough. Never be satisfied. I want to hold her forever, but my body has other plans. I ache to sink my teeth into her, bury my cock deep within her wet folds, and claim her in the most intimate way a man can have a woman.

It still won't be enough.

Try as I might for restraint, I fail. With a moan, I lean forward and sink my teeth into the soft skin below her ear, giving a slight nip. She arches back, exposing her neck. Her hands go around me and a soft warbling moan escapes her mouth. Such an angelic sound, it vibrates in the air and stirs my cock to life.

The woman is undeniably sensual in every breathy moan and every sweep of her tongue over lips I can't wait to claim next.

My heart sings, filled with an indescribable happiness, a sense of completion, something I don't believe and am afraid to accept. I hold her tight, one hand dipping down to cup her ass.

Not shy about what she wants, Dani grinds against me, moving in harmony with my need. We slide into a slow easy grind, and I love the way the arching of her back fits her pelvis so perfectly against my rigid erection.

We have on too many clothes, but I'm in no rush to rectify that situation. Dani's not a conquest. She deserves a more tender touch and I intend to worship every bit of her as long as I hold her in my hands.

I nip at her neck, laying a trail of kisses up the gentle sweep of tender flesh. I explore along the sculpted ridge of her jaw. Eventually, my nips and licks end with my lips hovering over hers.

"Dani, you taste like sin."

She giggles, and I wish it wasn't so dark, because I want to see the flush of red color her cheeks. I grip her ass, tugging her tight against me.

"You taste like something dangerous," she admits with a coy grin.

I pause. "Are you afraid of me?"

"I should be. I don't really know you."

"Are you sure about that?" I feel like I've known her my entire life. As if she's always been waiting for me. "Because it feels like I've known you forever."

Her lips part on a sigh and she tilts her head back. "It does, doesn't it? How can that be?"

I don't know, except there's far too much talking going on. Chest to chest, hips to hips, and mouth to mouth, I kiss her with my entire being. She kisses me back, and I feel her joy in the smile curving her lips.

Kissing takes over and the world around us disappears. The synergy of our connection explodes, fueled by the heat of our lips and the panting of our combined breaths. The round globes of her ass fit my palms perfectly and I hoist her off the ground.

Not missing a beat, she wraps her long legs around my hips, hooking her ankles over each other as she rests them on my ass. Nightfall comes and goes, leaving us in darkness except for the flickering shadows and faint light cast from my small fire. My bedroll is spread out on the dirt. Dynamo's already claimed his spot, and I consider taking the kiss to its logical conclusion.

Something holds me back.

I want to bring our bodies closer, obliterate any remaining space between us. I shove my tongue into the heat of her mouth and hold back a groan as I imagine doing the same with my cock. When I do, I'll never want to leave her sweet heat.

Dani is quickly becoming an addiction I don't want to quit.

The sounds of the night grow louder. Crickets rub their legs together, beginning their nighttime chorus of chirps and clicks. Somewhere off in the distance, cattle low and a night owl hoots. The wind rustles through the grass, mimicking the sound of an ocean thousands of miles away. Overhead, blackness blankets the sky and stars pierce the darkness with their weak, but steady glow.

I stand firmly on the ground, rooted to the earth. With a grip on the firm roundness of her ass, I kiss her with a fiery passion I've never experienced before.

I allow one hand to trail up the expanse of her back. The roughness of my calloused hands skims across buttery perfection. I reach the clasp of her bra and unhooked it with a deft flick of my fingers.

She gasps and lifts herself. The heat of her pussy presses against me, leaving me to gasp as well. With her bra no longer a barrier between us, I slip my hand around until the soft pillowy flesh of her breast fills my hand.

"You're so perfect, Dani."

Indeed, her perky breasts seem to have been made for me. A perfect handful, she's neither too small nor too large. I cup her breast in the palm of my hand, lightly squeezing as I acquaint myself with every inch of perfection. A soft mewling sound escapes her when I find her nipple. The tight little nub pebbles beneath the graze of my thumb.

With any other woman, I would've ripped off her shirt and divested her of her pants by now. I'd be balls deep inside of her.

For Dani, I hold off.

"Is this really happening?" Dani kisses my lips and draws back. Her doe-brown eyes shimmer in the flickering firelight.

Is it?

I haven't decided how far the evening will go. It'll take but a second to rid us both of the offensive clothing keeping me from my ultimate goal.

"Is that what you want?" I stare into her eyes, looking not for permission, but whether it'll be something she might regret in the morning. Heat and passion are all well and good, and lord knows we have enough of that simmering between us. The air crackles and pops with the energy coursing along my skin, but it isn't enough for me.

Her gaze pins me in place, slamming into my gut until it sucks out my breath.

Her tight nod gives me the permission I need to take everything I want, but there's something in her eyes which holds me back. A hesitancy I need to resolve.

"I want nothing more than to fuck you right here, but I don't want any regrets. We don't have to do this. There will be plenty of time for more later. This is happening between us, but it doesn't need to happen tonight."

"It doesn't?"

"No, luv. It doesn't."

"You don't want to…" Her questioning gaze travels over my face, beginning at my eyes and ending on my lips. Confusion fills her expression where it mingles with doubt. She worries her lower lip between her pearl-white teeth, looking vulnerable and suddenly unsure. My girl is cooling off and it's all my fault.

"Here." I take her hand in mine and place it over my straining cock. "I want nothing more than to slip inside of you and spend all night making you come on my cock. I'm painfully aroused and, honestly, I'm going to need some relief before I bust a nut, but not at the expense of any regrets."

"I won't regret sleeping with you."

"Are you sure?"

"I think so." Her brows pinch and her gaze slips.

I shift my stance and ever so slowly set her back on the ground. I keep a hand wrapped around her waist and brush my lips over hers, stealing another kiss. With a low groan, I pull back.

"I'm not sure if an '*I think so*' is going to be enough for me."

"Are you saying you don't want to have sex?" Confusion marches across her face, followed by a slice of indignation.

"Does this feel like me not wanting to fuck?" I keep her hand pressed against my hard length straining against my zipper.

"But? I don't get it." Her long lashes flutter over the high arch of her cheekbones. The firelight makes the movement sultry and magical.

"I can hardly breathe, Dani." I admit a difficult truth. "You do that to me. And I very much want to toss you to the ground and fuck until we both pass out from exhaustion, but not at the expense of ruining this before it even begins. I'm not looking for one night between your legs. I'm looking for more."

I want a lifetime.

"I've never had a guy put on the brakes. That's supposed to be the girl's job." She gives a soft laugh full of complex thoughts I don't understand, but I'll unravel them.

I have forever to get inside her head.

"I can tell you this is a first for me." Tough to admit, but it's true. Usually the girl puts on the brakes, rarely the guy. And for me, that never happens. If there was pussy I wanted, I took it. No girl ever refused a chance with me. "If you were anyone else, you'd be on your third orgasm for the night."

"Third?" She looks like she doesn't believe me. "That kind of thing doesn't really happen. I'm not impressed by bravado."

It's my turn for a long slow blink. "Who the hell have you been sleeping with that doesn't give you at least two orgasms a night? Three is a minimum for me. That's not bravado, hun, it's truth."

She bites her lower lip and leans back.

"Dani, do you orgasm when you have sex?"

She blinks and looks away.

I grip her chin and force her to face me.

"I'm going to say a few things here you may or may not be comfortable with, but these are truths we're going to embrace."

"I..." Tension rises within her, evidenced by a slight lifting of her shoulders and the way she tries to pull away.

"No, it's best to talk this shit out first."

Her response is to stare at me, then shift her gaze away. She doesn't believe me, or she's never actually talked about sex with any of her previous boyfriends. There really is a lot we don't know about each other.

"First off, we talk about sex. Every bit of it. I want to know what you like, what you don't like, what turns you on, what turns you off, and what all your freaky little fantasies are that you've never told anyone before. It's just you and me. And between us, there are no secrets when it comes to sex. There's nothing to be ashamed of, nothing to fear. Sex is something we share together. It's not something where I take and you give. Any man who does that, or did that to you, isn't a real man. He's a selfish bastard who doesn't deserve you."

"Not everyone is like you."

Isn't that the truth? Few people dedicate their lives, or place their lives on the line for others. And too few men truly care about the sexual satisfaction of their partners. I push, because I want to make certain she understands.

"I've been with other women and you've been with other men. We don't need to talk specifics about any of that except to share what we know we like and what we've learned that we don't like."

"I'm not really comfortable talking about this." She covers her face with the long lengths of her hair, hiding from the scrutiny of my gaze.

I stoop to get eye-level with her. It is important she understands a fundamental truth.

"You will be with me. Given time, of course. Every filthy fantasy in that head of yours is something you'll share. Every fear. Every revulsion. All of it. The good. The bad. The ugly. There's nothing more intimate than baring your soul, and I intend to see all of you. Which is why we don't need to rush this. If you're not comfortable talking about sex, there's no reason to rush into having it."

"But what about…" She makes a vague gesture toward my cock.

"I'll rub one out after you leave." I shrug like it's nothing; only it's everything. I'd rather spend my night buried in her sweet heat rather than jerking off with my hand.

Her eyes widen and a tiny gasp escapes her, then she looks up at me with surprise.

"I take it you're not used to other men saying something like that either?"

"I'm not comfortable with this whole conversation. Talking isn't something I usually do when trying to have sex."

"Well, you need to get over that."

"I feel bad about…"

"My erection?"

She squirms in my arms.

"Can you not even say the word?" A huge grin spreads across my face.

"Dax…" She shies away from an answer.

"I want to hear you say it."

"I'm not saying it."

"Erection." I laugh. "Say it. You feel bad about leaving me with a raging hard-on. My cock is about to burst."

She dissolves into a fit of giggles and I love the laughter spilling from her mouth. It floats on the evening breeze and fills the air with everything wonderful about her. I'm beginning to love everything about Dani Studer. That should scare me, but I don't give a shit about that. It feels right.

I settle us on the ground and feed the flames of the campfire. There will be no sex tonight, but I do want to spend time with her.

I hold Dani, cuddling with her beside the fire while we search for shooting stars, howl at the moon, and track the movement of satellites from horizon to horizon. Dani's sweet scent infiltrates my senses and she slowly becomes a part of me.

We talk.

A lot.

If I did what my body demanded, there wouldn't be any talking and I would've missed out on the chance to get to know a little more about the woman in my arms.

She's smart. Incredibly intelligent, her sharp wit and zany comebacks to my jokes surprise me. When I point out the satellites, I expect nothing more than an *Oh, that's pretty!* Instead, she talks about animal experiments NASA has ongoing on the space station and tells me all about the first animals sent into space.

I ask about her degree, what lead her to consider veterinary medicine, and about her hopes for the future.

She and Dynamo fall in tight together. Instead of curling up with me, Dynamo expresses a definite preference for the girl. I can't blame the dog. I have a definite preference for the girl as well.

Not sleeping with her may be the hardest thing I've ever done in a very long time, but with her father's overprotectiveness, it makes sense. Tom Studer caught a glimpse of me kissing his daughter. If he knew all the ways I intend to defile Dani, I'll find myself staring down the barrel of a shotgun.

Studer can fire me.

I can't have that, because there's no way I'll leave Crowbar ranch, not unless it's with Dani by my side.

I can't remember the last time I didn't sleep with a woman on the first date. Going slow has never been my style. Hell, most times there was no date. When I felt the urge to blow off a little steam, cheap hookups were my modus operandi. Women who were overly eager to bang a man in special ops didn't care about anything other than how I performed in the sheets. One night worked out for all involved.

I used them. They used me. Everyone went their separate ways in the morning.

With predawn twilight pushing away the blackness of night, I find myself amazed by my restraint. It would've been too easy to move too fast. Unfortunately, the dawn brings work, and I still have my boss's daughter in my arms.

I shake her gently awake.

"Dani, wake up."

She stretches and looks up with sleepy eyes.

"What time is it?"

I check my watch, even though my body knows the rhythms of the day. It's not much past four am.

"Early, and we need to get you back to the house. If you're father knows where you spent the night…"

"Don't worry about him."

"You don't work for him, and I don't want to have to answer the question of what I may, or may not, have been doing to his daughter all night."

"He'll understand."

"He'll fire my ass." I lift her and lightly swat her ass. "Now, get. Go!"

She spins around, her hair in disarray, looking even more glorious in the predawn twilight. "Did you just tell me to *get* like a dog?"

I snicker. "You know I didn't mean it like that, but yeah. You need to get your ass in gear and get home before your dad wakes up. I don't need him riding my ass all day. We have to load up the bull and take it to Peace Springs."

She gives a little clap. "That's right. It's the Spring Fair. I want you to promise to ride the Ferris wheel with me."

"Dani, I'm going to be busy with your father."

She flaps a hand. "Don't worry about my dad. I know how these things go. Once you put the bull in the pen, there's not much for you to do. He'll take care of his bull business, which leaves you to take care of me."

"I don't think that would look good."

"Look, I don't really care how it looks, and I'll break it to my dad. He saw us kiss, and I already told him I like you."

"You did?"

"Yup."

"When?"

"After the whole trying to fall off a cliff thing. Don't worry about my dad. Leave him to me."

"I will, but only if you get home ASAP. I really don't want to explain what we were doing out here all night long."

"You won't have to." She leans forward and gives me a kiss. "Trust me."

She isn't the one I'm worried about. I give her a kiss, lift her into Honey's saddle and swat the mare in the ass to get her moving. Dani looks over her shoulder and blows me a kiss.

It pierces me right in the heart, taking my breath away.

SEVENTEEN

Dani

_____

THE EARLY MORNING AIR FLUTTERS AGAINST MY SKIN, BUT THAT ISN'T what brings chills shivering down my spine, or the static charge lifting the fine hairs of my arms. I wrap my arms around myself, letting go of Honey's reins, and give myself a hug.

I still smell him. Taste him. All of Dax's yummy goodness wraps me in a comforting blanket of never-felt-this-good-ever.

Honey doesn't need to be led back to the barn. The horse knows exactly where to go, and I let the horse lead while my thoughts spin with everything Dax related. Specifically, I imagine everything he promised.

The inevitability of sex lingers between us. I was taken aback when he put the stops on having sex, and then he blew my mind telling me we would talk about sex.

About everything to do with sex.

Everything.

I squirm in the saddle. How am I supposed to talk about something like that? With him? Scott never wanted to talk.

I take in a slow breath and fill my lungs with the promise of a new day, and more. It was the most perfect, most romantic, most seductive evening I've ever spent with a man before.

And no sex.

That still floors me.

Every movement Dax made was tense and calculating. All that power bunched in his muscles spoke about the sexual prowess he restrains. I sense a dangerous lethality within him, and yet, in his arms, I felt protected and safe.

He kisses with his entire being. Scott never did that. Scott barely kissed me at all, and when he did it was with wet, fish-mouth lips. Slobbery comes to mind.

Dax's lips felt like velvet, a smooth glide of tantalizing wonder hinting at pleasure to come.

Three orgasms in one night?

Dax speaks about it as if it's normal. He said *at least* three.

But that can't be true.

It has to be male bravado.

Scott barely got me to orgasm at all, and pretty much left it up to me to ensure I got off. He never said anything outright, but he made it clear if I didn't come before he was done he wasn't putting any additional effort into it. I thought it was like that with everyone.

Dax suggests otherwise.

He looked at me with the same shock I showed him. And he says we were going to talk about sex?

Scott never wants to talk about sex, and hates it when I suggest he might be able to do anything that could make the whole experience better for me. In many ways, Scott made me feel broken. As if my lack of orgasmic ability was due to a fault within my body, rather than something he could work on and improve.

"Danielle?" The deep rumbly voice of my father startles me and I jolt in the saddle. A quick grab to the pommel keeps me in the seat.

I'm so deep in thought, I didn't realize Honey meandered up to the barn.

"Daddy?" I sit stiffly in the saddle, waiting for him to connect the dots about where his daughter was and what I may have been up to.

"It's awfully early for you to be out and about. Did you have problems sleeping?"

He doesn't seem to know I didn't sleep in my bed. Or, maybe he does and this is a test?

"I was restless."

"It's been a long time since you took Honey out so early. Is everything all right?"

"Just had things to think about. I'm good."

He pulls a face. "I know I came down on you pretty hard about Scott. I don't mean to sound like I don't care. You deserve the best in a husband. I want you to know I'll be talking to him."

"I know you're looking out for me, and I appreciate it, even when I don't agree with it, but you don't need to talk to Scott."

He vents a deep sigh. The chilly air coalesces on his breath, forming a tiny vapor cloud.

"It's the curse of being a parent. We never know when to let go. As far as Scott is concerned…"

"I don't want to talk about Scott." I can't endure another moment thinking about a man who is firmly out of my life. Not when I have one camped out by the river who promises to open up a world of possibility.

"Okay, hun." He scratches at his jaw. "Are you going in to Peace Springs for the fair?"

"I was thinking about it. Cate invited me over for dinner. Do you need any help?"

"I can always use help, but I've got Dax to help me."

The way he says it sounds like a message. Dax will be with him, under my father's strict eye, and therefore not available to spend time with his daughter. That's okay. I can be incredibly persuasive when I want something.

"I really don't mind. You can always use a third hand."

"I appreciate it, but the two of us can handle it. I think spending some time with Cate might be perfect. You need to blow off a little steam."

Right, and not with the man he watched me kiss on horseback. I understand my father, but won't let him stand in our way.

"I can still drive down with you."

"You don't need to do that. We're going early and coming back just as early. I think the first calf might drop in the next day or two."

"That's exciting. I'd love to be there. You never know when you need an aspiring vet to help out."

Calving season might be a busy time of year, but the calves born now are the lifeblood of the ranch later when we go to market.

He puts his hands on my cheeks and kisses my forehead. "You're too enthusiastic, and it's not like it's the first calf you've ever seen delivered. I've got the bull loaded and I'm just waiting on Dax. We'll be gone before you have time to freshen up. While I appreciate your help, this is your break. Go have fun with your friends. You don't get many opportunities to see Cate."

It looks like my father is drawing a hard line in the sand with Dax, putting up barriers and obstacles no matter what I try. Maybe a direct approach will be more productive?

"About Dax..." How am I going to broach the subject about Dax with my father and not get Dax into trouble? Or fired?

My father has a way of ferreting out all my secrets, even when I don't know I have anything to hide. The last thing I need is for him to know I spent the night in Dax's arms, or that we talked about sex.

"Dax is none of your concern."

That isn't true.

"But..."

He holds up a hand. "We're not talking about him. I understand why you might see something in him, but your emotions are a little raw after what Scott did. You won't be the first girl to seek comfort in another man's arms after a breakup. Just remember what I said. Dax isn't for you, and he won't be around past calving season. Don't ruin your future today over something you'll regret tomorrow. You're engaged to Scott."

There's no thinking, or deciding. Scott and I are done. My father will come around and accept it eventually. Until then, I'll keep my thoughts about Dax to myself.

"I'm going to put Honey up and take a shower. Are you sure there's nothing you need my help with?"

If I can convince my father to let me go with him, he'll see the two of us together. As astute as he is, maybe he'll stop mentioning Scott and consider another possibility. He'll see that we're in love.

My father's words make up my mind, and although I rush through my shower, he leaves without me. That means Dax is with him.

Dax never said he would take me to the fair, or take that ride on the Ferris wheel. He didn't say *No* either. All I need is to get him away from my father long enough to enjoy the day and sneak in something more than a kiss.

My dad doesn't need Dax to return with him. It doesn't take two men to unload a bull into a pasture, which will give me the perfect opportunity to take Dax to Cate's for dinner. It can work.

Since my father left, I take a little more time with my appearance because I want to blow the socks off Dax when he sees me. It'll be impossible for him to refuse when I force him to go on the rides and steal kisses when no one's looking.

Two hours later, I park the Jeep in a field with a couple hundred other vehicles. Most are trucks and farm vehicles with trailers attached. There are other four-wheel vehicles, but also a smattering of sedans. This is a big day in Peace Springs, a time for the community to come out after a long winter and reconnect.

As with most fairs, it's a place for farmers to gather, buy seeds, check out the latest and greatest new farming toys. The ranchers are well represented with a smattering of heifers, bulls, and those young calves they're willing to trade.

Our bull will be put up for stud contracts, a way to improve the diversity of all the local herds. My father is likely looking at other bulls while he's here. The 4-H club represents well, with kids showing off their lambs, piglets, colts and calves that are a part of their projects.

Colorful booths line the main fairgrounds, full of funnel cakes, shaved ice, beer, hotdogs and all manner of scrumptious foods. The women are out with their quilts and pies, vying for the honor of being heralded the best of the best. And then there are the rides.

I love the rides. There really are no favorites. I enjoy the slow, sedate kiddy rollercoasters with as much enthusiasm as the Tilt-a-Whirl, bumper cars, Scrambler, and of course the Ferris wheel which takes eager ride-goers high up into the air where we can look down on all the merriment below us.

I text Cate.

ME: *I'M AT THE FAIR. WHERE RU?*

Cate: Running behind. Be there soon.

Me: Dax is here!

Cate: Awesome. Dinner?

Me: I'm trying. There may be a problem.

Cate: ???

Me: Dad.

Cate: I'll help.

I CAN COUNT ON CATE. GIVEN THE RIGHT PRESSURE, MY FATHER will cave. Now, where is he hanging out? Because Dax will be right by my father's side.

The animal pens are far back from the rides and vendor craft booths. I wander around the stalls of amazingly talented artisans displaying their crafts, mouth-watering food booths, and rides I can't wait to get on.

Little kids tug at their mother's skirts and dance around their father's legs, eager to get tickets to ride the best rides. Parents juggle plates laden with food, trying to feed their youngsters and themselves without dropping it all.

I weave through the crowd and soon the wonderful aroma of funnel cakes, cotton candy, and chili cookouts fades behind me to be replaced by the more pungent, earthy smells of livestock.

It's a big fair. Important for farmers and ranchers alike. Everyone has come out to see what their neighbors have been up to over the past few months. I work my way past the piglet racing booth, watch baby chicks waddle around in small boxes. I stop by an egg laying pen where a prize will be given for the largest egg laid during the fair.

Unlike those around me, I don't stop to gossip and catch up. Peace Springs isn't my town, and I don't recognize anyone from Bear Creek.

I do eventually find my way to the stalls holding the bulls being put up for stud auction. It doesn't take long before I find my father, because the overwhelming presence of Dax standing by his side takes my breath away.

From across the pen, his gaze lifts, as if he senses my presence. His lips turn up into the most magnificent smile. The angular scar tugs at his cheek, making him look ferocious and deliciously dangerous.

I know he isn't. The man has a heart of gold and a soft spot in it for me. I lift my hand to wave at Dax. Right at that moment, my father turns around. He catches me mid-wave and his hard gaze shifts to the man standing beside him. A frown darkens his face and turns into a grimace.

My father says something and Dax bows his head to listen. A second later, Dax shoulders his way through the crowd, heading away from me. I debate whether to go after him, but my father calls me to his side.

I weave though the thick crowd. Lifting on tiptoe, I give a peck to his cheek.

"How's it going, daddy?"

"Good, lots of good prospects. What are you doing here? I thought you were meeting up with Cate?"

"I am. She's running late."

He reaches into his pocket and peels off a handful of bills. When he tries to hand them to me, I put out my hand.

"You don't need to do that."

He shoves the money at me. "Humor me. I don't have too many opportunities to spoil my girl." His attention shifts in the direction Dax went. "You're growing up too fast."

I take the money, fold it, and shove it deep into my pocket. Glancing down at the hard-packed dirt, I slide my toe over the ground.

"Where did Dax go?" I know he sent Dax away, trying to keep us apart.

"Just an errand. Don't pay him any mind." He turns me around and gives me a little shove toward the front of the fairgrounds. "Now go have a funnel cake on me, and ride the rides you love so much."

"It's no fun riding alone."

"Cate will be here before you know it. Check out the booths and see if there are any gifts you want to bring back with you."

Gifts for whom? Although, I know. Despite my father's prodding, there's no way in hell I'm getting any kind of gift for Scott. I know a dismissal when my father gives it and look over the crowd, searching for Dax. A big man, he towers over everyone, but I don't see him. My father must have sent him some distance on whatever phony errand he concocted.

I walk dejectedly back to the main fairgrounds, hands shoved deep in my pockets, scuffing my feet, when a strong hand grips my arm and pulls me between two booths.

EIGHTEEN

Dani

WARM VELVETY LIPS SILENCE MY YELP AS DAX'S KISS CRASHES DOWN on my mouth. My eyes round, surprised by Dax's sudden appearance. Not that it matters. Nothing matters when he holds me in his arms.

I wrap an arm around his neck and struggle to resist the urge to climb his body in public. There's little protection from prying eyes, which may be the only reason he doesn't take the kiss further than I want. As far as I'm concerned, the crowd doesn't exist.

My skin itches. My clothes restrict my movement. I need to feel him skin to skin, and I shamelessly grind against him, needing friction and warmth, and a connection I can't describe.

Dax's body presses against mine, hard planes of muscle merging with my softer parts. His hands dip down to cup my ass and he yanks me against his groin. The long, swollen length of his erection tents his jeans and pushes against my belly. I giggle beneath the kiss.

Dax pulls back. "I'm not used to giggles, sweets. Breathy moans and my name as you come are what I prefer."

"You haven't made me come yet." I can't help it, but an impish smile creeps across my face.

"Is that a challenge?" The arch of his brow indicates he's on board for such a thing.

I bite my lower lip and lift on tiptoe to whisper into his ear. "Erection."

His entire body stills and he huffs a laugh. "Seems our conversation has given you something to think about. I love your filthy mouth."

My stomach flutters. Our conversation emboldens me.

It feels weird actually saying the word. Not that I've never said it before. But I certainly never said it to a man I want to fuck.

"Do you know what I want to do with my very erect cock?" His mischievous eyes twinkle.

"I can think of a thing or two." Did those words just escape my mouth? I don't know this wanton thing I become around Dax. Where is the shy, introverted, sexually repressed woman I know so well?

Dax makes talking about sex seem natural. Fun even. Is it?

It takes a long hard second to answer that question. There's no denying he makes the entire idea of sex sound fun. It's a game, an intimate expression between the two of us. Something without judgement where I find the freedom to explore.

Fairgoers pass us by, taking a long look at the couple engaged in an amorous embrace. Public displays of affection aren't exactly frowned upon, but they aren't encouraged in the largely religious crowd.

Dax's voice deepens, turning raw and rough. He stoops to whisper in my ear. "I want to shove my cock between your pretty lips, feel the rasp of your tongue as you lick me into oblivion, and I want the tip of my cock bouncing at the back of your throat as I come."

My entire body stills. "Um, that's quite a visual."

"Do you want to know what I want to do with *my* tongue."

Warmth spreads out from my core and throbs between my legs. I pinch my thighs together but it does nothing to ease the steady ache.

"Dax…"

"I want to lick your pussy and taste you as you come on my face. I want to shove my fingers deep inside your wet heat until your throat is hoarse from screaming my name. I want to take my cock—"

I place my hand over his mouth and look over my shoulders. Surely someone heard that last part. The growl in his voice grows louder with each dirty thing he says.

Behind my hand, a huge grin splits his face. His electric blue eyes twinkle with mischief and a very real promise.

"Too much?" He kisses my fingers and pulls my hand away from his mouth.

"That was a little intense." Overwhelmingly intense. I've never had a man speak to me about such things, and never about what he wants to do to me.

People don't really talk like that. Do they?

The features of his face smolder with the passion he has yet to unleash. "Hun, you have no idea what you're in store for do you?"

"I think I'm way out of my league."

"Don't be afraid, we're going to get to know everything about each other, beginning with how I like my blowjobs and how I'm absolutely going to love eating you out."

I can't help it. That comment has me squirming in place. No one's ever expressed an interest in eating me out. Not with that kind of hunger.

Isn't it kind of gross?

Scott seems to think so. He never volunteers to do *that*. But Dax speaks of it with an unrequited hunger. Like he really wants to...*do that!*

I give a low throaty moan, and struggle to regain control of our conversation. What were we talking about?

"What no real sex?" It isn't much of a deflection, but it's the best I can do...considering.

"You think that's not real?" He draws back. "Do you doubt that's what I want to do?" He cocks his head and gives me a look. "You have no idea how much I want to taste you."

"Um..." I'm trying to play things cool, as if men say this kind of thing to me all the time, but it makes me feel uncomfortable.

He laughs, a deep honest chuckle. "I have so much to show you, and I can't wait to begin. I rubbed one out after you left this morning. I can't stop thinking about fucking you." His attention sweeps across the crowd. "But this is not the place for that. Meet me tonight. Same place? Can you do that?"

"Depends on why you want me there?" Does he intend to fuck me, or hold me and watch shooting stars cross the heavens?

A rhetorical question, I know exactly what he intends. Things between us move at supernatural speed. An unstoppable eventuality, we're a combustible force of nature. And while I've never had a one night stand in my life, sleeping with Dax after what amounts to a day, or two at most, doesn't feel wrong.

It feels...inevitable.

He gives me a wink. "I figure we'll talk until my dick gets hard. I'll lick you until you come, finger you for a bit, then we'll discuss your fear about giving blowjobs."

"My what?" I didn't say anything about blowjobs. They may not be my favorite sexual act in the world, but how did he pick up on that?

He bends down and sweeps a chaste kiss across my lips. His voice lowers, turning sinfully dark, lusty, but more importantly, his words make me feel safe and secure, like I can trust him with all of my insecurities. He'll never force anything on me.

"You're an open book to me. I see every thought in your head." He points to his chest. "Every doubt and insecurity, I feel it right here. You can't hide from me, but don't worry. We'll conquer your fears together, beginning with me eating your pussy."

I squirm at that comment and shift away from him. He pulls me back to him.

"Are you sure about that?" I can't help the insecurity lacing my words.

Perhaps my sexual experiences with Scott stunted me. He was my first and only sexual partner. Of course, I read books, see things online, and talk about stuff with my girlfriends, but I only know what I know.

For me, sex is something I give away. It's not something I enjoy. That's all I know. Dax seems to think sex is something more of a give and take, but I worry I won't be able to give him what he needs.

What will happen when we're finally alone and Scott is right? What if there is something wrong with my body? Something broken? What if sex isn't something I'll ever enjoy?

Dax takes my hand in his and leads me out from the relative privacy between the two vendor stalls.

"I want to take you on that Ferris wheel you keep talking about."

"You don't have to do that." I glance back toward the livestock pens. "Isn't my dad waiting on you?"

"Don't worry about that."

But I do. I worry about everything. Scott says I'm high strung, high maintenance, and need to chill out. I doubt everything.

The enthusiasm with which Dax pulls me along becomes infectious. A quick stop at a ticket booth and he buys enough tickets for us to ride every ride.

"Don't you need to get back to my dad?"

"He's not expecting me for a while. We have plenty of time to ride your Ferris wheel." He tugs me along and I follow with a lightness in my step.

Despite the crowds, the lines to the rides move quickly. Before I know it, the ride operator takes our tickets and lowers the safety bar to our chair. Dax leans close and whispers into the man's ear, then shakes his hand.

"I don't think I've seen you smile that bright." Dax leans over and gives me a quick peck on the cheek as the Ferris wheel moves. Our chair lifts into the air, but then comes to a halt with a slow rock as the people in the car behind us exit and another group climbs in.

It's a perfect day with bright blue skies, puffy clouds, and weather which manages to cooperate. In springtime, fickle Montana weather brings bright sunny days such as this, where only a light jacket is needed, to plunging temperatures and surprise blizzards. Today is one of the good days.

We work our way up to the top of the Ferris wheel until all the chairs are reloaded with eager riders. Dax and I rock in our seat as I stare down on the fair.

"Have you been to many county fairs?" I lean forward, loving the view, and grin with my childhood memories.

The last time I was on a Ferris wheel my father sat beside me. Scott thinks rides and game booths are lame. He came home with me our freshman year to meet my father and I forced him to go to the fair. The two of us spent more time at the livestock pens, and Scott seemed much more interested in talking to my father than spending time with me.

The two of them hit it off immediately, which might be part of the reason my father is having such a hard time with the breakup. He's losing the son-in-law he already accepted into the family.

The Ferris wheel starts to spin, lowering us down then rushing us up over the crowd. I love the way my stomach drops as we fall and squeeze Dax's hand as I grin. He sits beside me, our arms brushing against each other, our fingers woven together, and a simmering promise building between us.

"All the time." He drapes his arm over my shoulders. "You could say I grew up with them. I love everything about them, the smells, the kids, the rides…" He gave my shoulder a squeeze. "Kissing girls at the top of the Ferris wheel."

"I bet there were a lot of lucky girls."

He shrugs. "None that matter now. You're the one I want, and you make me the happiest man in the world."

I lean against him, snuggling into the crook of his arm. "I kind of like you too."

"Well, shit, that's good to know."

The ride slows down and comes to a stop. We dangle over the crowd as the ride operator starts letting people off. When it comes for our turn to get out, the operator skips our car.

"What?"

Dax slips his arm down lower, tugging me tight against his body. He leans down and whispers. "I paid for a little extra time with my girl."

The heat of his breath feathers across my cheeks, then the warmth of his mouth finds mine. The entire world disappears beneath that kiss, and I believe there must truly be a heaven.

Dax bribed the operator, because we spend much longer at the apex of the ride than we should, but eventually all things must end. The ride lurches into motion and I curl my lower lip between my teeth, loving the sensual flavor of everything Dax.

He helps me out, lending a hand, then threads our fingers together as he leads me to a hotdog vendor. We eat hotdogs and I tease him by gliding my tongue around the tip of the hotdog. One indignant mother snorts at us, which sends me into a fit of giggles.

Dax laughs and pulls me away. "You are a very naughty girl, and don't think I won't forget that."

"Forget what?" I bat my eyes at him, playing coy, but let my gaze linger on the prominent bulge behind his zipper.

"What that pretty mouth will be doing later tonight."

We finish our hotdogs and Dax pulls me into a hug.

"I have to get back. Your father is probably wondering what's keeping me." He gives me a quick kiss, much too light, and much too brief, then releases me to spin around and head back to the livestock pens at a jog.

I give a deep sigh, not believing this incredible thing is happening between me and Dax. It can't be real, but I'm beginning to believe in true love.

Someone grips my arm...hard.

Before I can yank free, I'm pulled off my feet. I spin, ready to give the asshole a piece of my mind, then stop dead in my tracks.

"Scott?" My heart slams into my throat.

Rage fills Scott's face.

"What are you doing here?" My words sound pathetic, weak, and scared.

"I might ask you the same. Who the hell was that guy?" Scott's grip tightens on my arm and he pulls me toward the parking lot.

"What are you doing? Let go." I try to jerk out of his grip, but his hand clamps down on my upper arm.

"You and I need to have a talk." His gaze casts in the direction Dax went. "I don't know who the hell that guy was, but whatever is going on, it ends now."

"Look, you don't get to tell me what I can or can't do, or who I can and can't do it with. If you remember, we're no longer engaged. Now, let me go."

His teeth grind together and the muscles of his jaw bunch. "Not until after we talk."

"There's nothing to talk about." I dig in my heels, but Scott gives a hard yank. I stumble as he drags me through the crowd. "So help me if you don't let go right now, I'll scream."

"You don't want to do that. It won't look good for either of us."

"There is no us." My shout draws the attention of those closest to us.

Scott stops and spins me around. His free hand cups my jaw. His fingers dig into the soft tissues of my cheeks, making me sputter. Leaning in, he drops his voice to a harsh whisper.

"I swear, if you make a scene, you'll regret it."

"Or what?" I grip his wrist, trying to peel his hand off my jaw.

"Or you won't like what happens next."

"Don't you dare threaten me."

"Dani…" My entire body stills at the sound of my father's voice. "Please. There are things we need to discuss. Let Scott take you home. I'll explain everything tonight."

"I'm not going home with him. I'm not going anywhere with Scott."

My father draws in a deep breath. "Honey, I need you to listen, and I need you to do as you're told."

"I'm not a little girl…"

"No, but you are my daughter. Danielle…"

My father is the only person who ever uses my full name. It's used with the greatest respect and the tenderest love. He never raises his voice to me in anger, but that name always gets my full and complete attention. He needs me to listen.

My father clears his throat. "Trust me. Everything is going to work out. I need you to listen. Scott and I…we talked things out." He gives a hard stare at Scott. "He won't hurt you." My father's gaze cuts to the vice-like grip Scott clamps around my arm.

Beneath my father's stare, Scott loosens his grip and releases my jaw. He doesn't let go of my arm.

"Daddy?" Why is he letting Scott hurt me?

"I'll be home just as soon as the bull is loaded. We'll discuss everything over dinner."

NINETEEN

Dax
———

I JOG BACK TO THE PEN WHERE STUDER'S BULL STANDS. TOM Studer asked me to look into a few select breeding arrangements. What he did was send me off when Dani arrived at the pens. Fortunately, I ran into Caleb, who introduced me to Drake, and the two of them handle things for me while I search for Dani.

Such a simple thing, taking her for a ride on the Ferris wheel, but I sense it means something more to her. Something special. After a career jumping out of planes for a living, rides at a fair do nothing for me.

Putting a smile on Dani's face?

That is everything.

I may be a thrill seeker, but no one can say I'm a romantic. I'm more of a don't-make-things-complicated-for-me kind of guy. With Dani, all that gets turned on its head.

I want to do special things for her because her reactions fill me with joy. They're pure and unfiltered, and that does funny things to my insides. It's not a sexual thing, but rather something much more profound.

The way her face beams when I put a smile on her face makes my heart thump in the best possible way. Her smiles are all the sustenance I need, and I'm suddenly aware of how empty my life was before she entered it.

All those nameless and cheap fucks are exactly that, a means for temporary physical release which in the end left me empty and hollow. Dani fills the emptiness inside of me. She makes me want to be more than a memory.

I weave my way through the crowd, one which slowly thins now that the auctions are closed.

One of the ranchers Studer introduced me to earlier in the day lifts his arm over his head when he sees me and waves me over.

"Hey there." I can't remember the guy's name. The man glances around, looking ready to get out of there. Most of the wheeling and dealing is done. I understand the man's eagerness to get back to work. The fair might be over, but there's still plenty to do.

"Hey Dax. Tom had to deal with something and asked me to load his bull. Since you're here…"

"Yeah, no problem. I've got it." I shake hands with the man and assure him I've got the bull in hand.

Some people might think leading a bull around by a tiny rope doesn't make any sense, but the ring in the bull's nose keeps it in check.

Honestly, bulls are surprisingly gentle creatures; at least when they aren't spooked or horny. Put a bull in a pasture with his cows, however, and all bets are off. Bulls are notoriously territorial and protective of their herds.

I lead the animal and it ambles along behind me, chewing its cud as its docile brown eyes take in all the humans. There are no cows to protect, so the bull remains steadfast and calm.

I lead the bull out the back of the pens and load him into the trailer behind Studer's pickup.

As I latch down the trailer gate, my cell phone buzzes. I wipe the dirt from my hands and fish my cell phone out of my pocket. A quick look at caller ID and I relax. My father's been trying to get a hold of me, and I'm not interested in talking.

The conversation is always the same and grates on my nerves.

Where are you?

When are you coming home?

Your mother misses you.

We need to talk.

It's because of that last one that I stopped taking my father's calls altogether. I know we need to talk, and we will…when *I'm* ready for it. Not when the imperious Seth Kingston demands it.

But the call isn't from my father. It's from my mother, and I'll never disrespect my mother by not talking her call.

"Hey mom. How are you doing?" Sweat beads my brow and I wipe off the perspiration with the back of my hand.

"I…" Her voice sounds stressed.

"Is everything okay?"

"Where are you?" There it is again. A tiny tremor.

Did my father put her up to this call? It would be just like him to leverage the relationship between mother and son.

My mother, however, refuses to get between the two of us. It's a line she never crosses.

If the next thing out of her mouth is, *When are you coming home,* I'll know whether my father pressured her into making this call.

"Just sorting things out." I try to deflect, seeing if my father's hand is indeed interfering in my relationship with my mother.

"I need you to come home."

It's not *"when are you coming home?,"* but pretty close. I prepare to defend my decision.

"We talked about this. I need a little time to sort a few things out before I come home, and no, I don't know how long that'll be. I promise, you'll be the first to know."

"No honey, I need you to come home now." Her voice cracks again, and a tiny sob escapes her normally calm composure. "I'm sending the jet, but I need to know where to send it."

Sending the jet? That's very unlike my mother and hints at an urgency she's yet to mention.

"What's wrong?"

My mother is the strongest woman I know, and she never loses her shit. Her stoic composure never once slips. Something has her rattled.

"Please, I—just tell me where you are. The pilots are on standby and ready for take off, but they need a destination to file the flight plan."

"Tell me what's wrong."

"I need you."

"Tell me what's wrong and we'll figure out how to handle it."

"Alexander Kingston," her voice rises in pitch, "if you don't tell me right now…" The use of my full name normally would've drawn my nuts up tight, but her soft sobs trailing at the end have me leaning forward and gripping the phone as if I can crawl through the connection to hold her in my arms.

I don't hesitate.

"Send it to Bozeman Montana. Wait, let me see if Peace Springs has an airport big enough for the jet."

Like all things, we do things bigger and better in Texas and that includes the family's personal jet. I haven't flown in it since leaving home, and don't understand the urgency behind my mother sending it. I can buy a regular ticket, like a regular guy.

Only, I'm not a regular guy.

My father calls me his legacy. The weight of our family's name weighs heavily on my shoulders.

Too heavy.

A quick check of the local airport reveals it's too small for the family jet to land. It needs to land in Bozeman.

I tell my mother where to send the jet. "Now, tell me what's wrong."

"It's your father…"

It takes a minute to figure out what's going on. Her voice cracks, becoming unintelligible, and I can't understand what's happening at first. But then it becomes all too clear. My father is in intensive care, in unstable condition, and they don't know if he'll make it through the night.

"I'm coming home."

"Thank you." It guts me that she thinks it necessary to thank me for coming home for what amounts to a family emergency. I still don't know what's wrong with my father. My mother is too distressed to explain.

I run a hand through my hair and debate my next move. I need to let Dani know I have to leave town. Our nighttime rendezvous needs to be postponed.

A few minutes later, Studer ambles up to the truck. He glances at me, brows pinched together.

"We ready to go?" Studer spits on the ground and another frown wrinkles his brow.

"Locked and loaded." I keep my voice smooth. My family's problems put a dent in Studer's ranching operations. That's something I regret. Studer's a solid, hard working man and I don't like leaving him in a lurch.

Somehow, I need to make my absence as painless as possible.

There is so much that Studer could benefit from, ways to turn the ranch profitable again, but it's too soon for me to suggest those changes. The man doesn't know me well enough, and I have yet to broach the subject of my ranching connections.

Maybe I can talk to my father and see about Kingston Ranch branching out? Studer can use the capitol investment, and it'll be a way to keep me near Dani, at least until she graduates. Then we can decide whether to stay in Montana, or move to Texas. I don't have a good feel on how attached Dani is to Montana, or her home. One way or the other, one of us needs to move.

As soon as I fly home, and figure out whatever is going on with my father, I'll return to finish out calving season, and present Studer with a proposal.

I give a low chuckle. There will likely be two proposals: one for business and one of a much more personal nature. Which reminds me to speak to my mother about my grandmother's ring.

Studer tosses me the keys and climbs into the passenger seat. The man looks like a great burden weighs on his shoulders. A deep scowl settles on his face, and I think little of it as we climb inside.

Knowing when to give a man space to wrestle with his demons, I say nothing. I drive back to the ranch while Studer stares out the passenger side window. The man looks more than troubled, he looks sick to his stomach, like he sacrificed a virgin to the devil.

I consider asking what's going on, but sense Studer needs space. Besides, we aren't buddies who sit around the campfire shooting the shit. Right now, I'm nothing more than a hired hand.

Soon, that power dynamic will shift.

Once Studer finds out my intentions with Dani everything will change. For one thing, I'll have to come clean about how I know as much as I do about cattle ranching.

Maybe that's a good thing.

Crowbar Ranch is a small operation compared to Kingston Ranch. Studer has some great ideas, but they're outdated and cost him money he can't afford to lose.

I leave the old man to his worries as I grip the wheel and let my thoughts drift to a more immediate issue.

My father.

My mother says my father is in intensive care. Unresponsive was one of several concerning words she used. As a certified paramedic, I know enough to worry, but I also understand how my mother might exaggerate. She doesn't understand medicine the way I do.

What she failed to mention is what landed my father in intensive care. In my haste, I didn't ask. All I know is that my father collapsed.

But why?

Was there an accident?

Heart attack? Stroke?

Like me, my father was born in the saddle and began his ranching career at the tender age of nine. My father never stopped, moving from high school to shouldering the burden of a legacy spanning generations.

I began much the same, following my father's footsteps as I learned everything there is to know about cattle and the business of ranching. But then, doubt crept in. Sometime during high school the urge to do more with my life stirred within me.

Enlisting in the Air Force was my way of defying my father. Like many young men, the urge to separate myself from the expectations of my family rose within me. I felt trapped, and suffocated beneath a burden I didn't want. I needed to discover the man I could be, rather than the one I was destined to become.

With an epic *Fuck You*, I left home, enlisted in the Air Force, and saved lives by risking mine.

The most rewarding job in the world, I made a difference rescuing wounded warriors and bringing them home… alive.

There was one mission, one I'll never forget. My team was called in to rescue the crew of a downed medievac helicopter. Two were members of the Army's equivalent of a medical evacuation special operations team, similar to Para-Jumpers. The third was the pilot.

A female pilot.

I still remember the tenacious Warrant Officer. Ariel Black pulled two injured medics out of her downed helicopter, while it was engulfed in smoke and flames, and before it exploded. As if that wasn't heroic enough, she did it with a busted up leg, and took a bullet in the process. She defended her position, holding off armed men, until my team arrived.

Guns blazing, we swooped in, neutralized the threat, and rescued the injured. It was just another day in the life of a Para-Jumper, but it meant the different between life and death for those three soldiers.

That's what I lived for. It's what I trained for. It's also the mission which ended my career. Like the pilot, I took a bullet and shrapnel from a grenade. Everyone made it out, but the trajectory of my career was irrevocably altered.

Worse, my injuries justified my father's anger. Putting my life on the line risked everything my father spent a lifetime to build. That began the great rift which separates us. My father doesn't understand why I risked my life, whereas I wouldn't have it any other way.

There are things in life which matter, and I need life to make sense. No matter the cost. No matter the personal price.

I need to do that now, swoop in and rescue my father, even knowing it's crazy.

This isn't an armed engagement.

My father isn't pinned down by hostile fire.

I can't save the day.

Not that it stops me from stepping on the gas pedal harder than I should. I push the limits of the truck with its trailer and prize bull inside, racing toward Crowbar Ranch.

I wish I could drive straight to Bozeman and meet the jet, but Dynamo is at the ranch. I can't leave without my dog.

Or my girl.

"You look troubled." Studer leans back in his seat and adjusts the seatbelt over his lap. He seems to have snapped out of his funk.

"I need to leave."

Studer says nothing for a time, merely shakes his head. After a few minutes, he lifts his hand.

"I appreciate the time you've given me. I hope you were able to sort out some of your issues."

I haven't. Crowds still make me anxious. Loud sounds don't bother me nearly as much as they used to. I handled the fair much better than I thought possible, but chalk that up to the presence of one person in particular.

I need to talk to Studer about Dani. When I return from Texas, I'll ask properly for Dani's hand in marriage. That's the kind of gesture Studer would appreciate.

"I'm not sure how long I'll be gone. I got some bad news about my father."

Studer stiffens in the seat. "Bad?"

"He's in the hospital." I take in a deep breath. "Intensive care. My mother doesn't know if he'll pull through."

"I'm very sorry to hear that. Of course, you need to go home. I appreciate all the help you've given me these past few weeks."

"I'm sorry to leave."

"It's okay. Family comes first and I'd never ask you to stay knowing you're needed at home." Studer gazes out the window and blows out his breath. "Managing this ranch doesn't get any easier. Each year seems worse than the last, but hopefully things will be looking up."

"Is that so?" I don't know how that can be.

Studer runs a tight operation, but he doesn't run enough cattle to make it profitable. Not with the wide swings in the market. It's something I've meant to mention, different ways to turn a profit on the ranch. When I return, I'll come clean with Studer about my background. I'll have to if I'm going to ask for Dani's hand in marriage.

"I'm finalizing a deal which will see to Dani's future," Studer says. "It means some changes, but hopefully they'll turn a profit on this land."

"Really?" My ears perk up. How do his business dealings affect Dani's future? "How so?"

"Worked out a deal with a local family. They say I'm sitting on a goldmine in mineral rights."

I don't like the sound of that. Whenever mineral rights are mentioned, it means devastation to the land.

I cover my mouth and cough. "Be careful with those kinds of deals. They're often not what you think."

"How is that?" Studer's brow lifts. "And not to be an ass, but how would you know?"

"I know a thing or two about deals like that. Not that I'm trying to stick my nose where it doesn't belong, but anything which strips the land is something that deserves careful consideration."

"I know what it means, but I don't have the luxury of waiting another season."

"Have you made the deal?"

"It's not finalized yet, but I'm thinking we'll move up the timetable. It depends on...well, it depends on some things." Pain stretches through Studer's words and something distasteful twists his mouth. Whatever this deal is, Studer doesn't like it.

"Maybe we can talk when I come back. I've been meaning to speak with you about a couple of things, actually."

Studer's pensive expression turns into a scowl. We pull down the lane and I stop outside the barn.

I hop out and offload the bull from the trailer.

Studer oversees my work, pulling at his face, the scowl deepening.

Once I get Dynamo and my things, I need to speak with Dani.

Gravel crunches beneath Studer's boots. "I see where your eye is gazing. My daughter...she's not for you."

"Sir, Dani and I..."

"I know what you're going to say, and I'm telling you it ends now. Dani has a life ahead of her, obligations she must meet, and she needs to focus on her future." He levels his steely gaze on me. "Not on someone who will put everything I've worked hard for at risk."

"Sir…" I was expecting a conversation along these lines, but not one with such finality.

"You said you needed to leave. I think it's a perfect time for you to pack your things and go."

"I'm not leaving without Dani."

Studer widens his stance. "I'm asking you to go quietly. I'll explain to Dani why you needed to leave."

There's no way that's happening. And I'm not about to get into a fight with her father. Studer is right about one thing. Dani has a life ahead of her, and it's a life with me by her side.

"I'll get my things, but I will see her."

"And ruin her future?" Studer gestures toward the house. "Her future is in there with the man she's going to marry. Your presence will only complicate matters."

The ground shifts under my feet, like the bottom dropped out from beneath me. "What did you say?"

"You heard me. Her fiancé is here. They've been through a bit of a rough patch, and I know Dani has allowed herself to be distracted. Whatever went on between the two of you, it means nothing."

"Nothing?"

"Look, I'm sorry to be the one to say it, but my daughter was simply blowing off a little steam. Which is why it's best that you leave. Don't come back. Dani needs to focus on her future, not some spring fling."

Something isn't right. Studer seems entirely too invested in Dani's love life. I know everything about the asshole who cheated on Dani and broke her heart. If that's the man her father wants her to marry, I will intervene.

What I won't do is make a scene. I have the distinct impression if I head toward the house, Studer will block me. Knocking down my future father-in-law doesn't seem like the right way to begin a life with Dani.

I allow my gaze to linger on the main house, then turn back to Studer. "That man in there broke your daughter's heart. Are you sure that's the kind of life you want for her?"

"There's more to it than that." Studer's shoulders hunch.

"You're right about that."

TWENTY

Dani

I sit on the couch, arms crossed and ankles pressed tight together. My teeth grind with righteous anger. Scott shoved me into my Jeep, after taking the keys away, and drove me home where he proceeded to drag me out of the vehicle and deposit me on the couch.

I haven't moved in nearly half an hour.

He lectures me about our future and promises I need to uphold.

I glare while he paces. When he turns his back, I stick out my tongue.

His hand shakes as he drags it through his dirty blond hair. I've never been afraid of him, but in the parking lot, I feared what he would do if I didn't get in the car. What will happen if I make a break for the door? Will he try to stop me? The four red marks on my arm says yes.

He notices the direction of my gaze and how my fingers trace over the bruising.

"Look," he says, "I'm sorry about that. I didn't mean to hurt you." He takes half a step toward me. When I draw back, he spins around and picks up his pacing.

"But you did." My attention shifts to the door, measuring how many steps it'll take and the chances of getting out of here.

But where will I go? Scott has the keys to my Jeep. I can make a break for the barn, but it takes time to saddle a horse. I can run, but Scott is faster. Until my father returns, I'm effectively a prisoner in my own home.

"I just needed to get your attention." His gaze lands on my arm again, and the marks he left behind.

"You had my attention, but it doesn't matter. You and I are done. Why is that so hard for you to accept?"

"We're not done. You need to understand that."

"You cheated on me." Seriously, I sound like a broken record.

"It's not like I planned on sleeping with Beth."

"How does that excuse what happened? You took me home and then you slept with her." My voice rises, filled with the pain and indignation of the whole series of events.

There was a time when I thought I loved Scott. Truthfully, before Dax, I didn't know what true love felt like. Scott felt *comforting*.

I did what was expected; go to college, date a boy, get engaged. Whatever Scott and I shared was a poor imitation of the feelings Dax brings about.

Dax feels like forever.

Maybe that isn't a good way to describe love. It isn't flowery, or something for a book of poems, but it feels right. There's a solidness with Dax. A sense of connection I never shared with Scott.

"I'm not excusing my behavior." His hand shakes as he runs it through his hair. He tugs at the roots and returns to pacing. "But it doesn't matter. It happened. It'll never happen again."

"I don't care if it does or doesn't happen again. I don't plan on being around to find out."

He stops. "But you will be around. It's been discussed."

"Discussed? Not by me."

"Your father arranged it."

"My father doesn't have the right to arrange anything. I'm not something that can be sold or traded." Did I miss something? A giant leap back in time? "I'm not chattel, Scott. You can't buy me."

"You're wrong about that."

Enough of his nonsense, I rise from the couch. My gaze darts to the door. In that split second, Scott closes the distance and pushes me back on the couch.

"You don't get it, but you will." He towers over me as I bounce on the springy cushions. "You belong to me."

"Don't you ever touch me like that again."

"I'll do that and more. I don't know what your father has, or hasn't said to you, but he's in default on all his loans. My family will cover them, and you won't lose your family's land, but only if we marry."

"That's crazy." It sounds very unlike my father. "Stuff like that doesn't happen." *Not in this day and age.* "And as far as the loan goes, I'll go to the bank and explain…"

"The loans are in default. As long as we're engaged, those payments are covered. Break the engagement and you and your father lose everything. Is that what you want?"

That isn't what I want at all. Where is my father? He'll sort all of this out.

"I don't believe you." I cross my arms over my chest, more to keep from trembling than out of anger or disbelief. Something my father said earlier about trying to fix things with Scott bothered me, and the way my father acted at the fair? It brings too many questions bubbling to the surface.

"Your father brokered a deal. This is happening."

"No, it's not. I don't love you. Hell, I don't even trust you."

"Your father and I talked. I made him a promise. What happened with Beth will never happen again. We're good together, Dani, and we'll be good again. You can't deny we've had good times." He goes to one knee. "I promise you'll have a good life, a secure life. Money will never be a problem. I'll even finance your practice, but only if you put my ring back on. And, we're not waiting until graduation. We'll finalize everything as soon as we can get the marriage certificate. I know you're mad, but this is for the best. I promise I'll make you happy."

"You're delusional."

"Am I? I pay off your family's debts. Your land stays in the Studer family. That's the concession your father made. All the details have been worked out."

"No one consulted me."

"No one needed to. It's a business arrangement. Things between us were going great, therefore there was nothing to worry about."

"Until you cheated on me." Cue the broken record.

Is he listening to a word I say?

"That has nothing to do with the terms of the arrangement."

"Why do you even care? Our ranch is small. It barely makes any money at all."

"It's been losing money for years."

I have no idea if that's true. My father doesn't share that kind of stuff with me.

"Then why the hell do you want it?"

"I don't care about ranching, silly, but this land is sitting on a fortune in mineral rights."

A coldness settles over me with the realization he wants to rape the land. Whatever loans my father has outstanding, Scott's family stands to make millions off the mineral rights. It's a sour deal and not something I can be a part of, but what about my father? He stands to lose everything.

The front door bangs open and Dax barrels in. He takes one look at Scott, then rushes to place himself between me and my very ex-fiancé.

"She's mine." Like an avenging angel, Dax's chest puffs out. His sheer size dwarfs Scott's shorter, blocky frame.

It's odd how I always thought Scott was a large man, but cowering before Dax's imposing presence, he seems somehow...less.

I jump off the cushion and place myself behind Dax. Feeling the tension in the room skyrocket, I thread my fingers in the belt loops of Dax's jeans and give a gentle tug.

"Get me out of here." My tiny voice sounds thready and weak, but I firm my lower lip and give another tug. Knowing what Dax is capable of, I don't want the two men throwing down in my living room.

Dax reaches back, placing his hand on my hip and takes a step back. We walk backwards, toward the door, when the floorboards of the porch creak. I turn and my jaw drops. Standing in the middle of the doorway, my father holds a shotgun and racks the slide, chambering a shell.

Dax spins. With his hand on my hip, he shifts me out of the line of fire. This places me behind him, open to Scott, but I guess he figures my father is the greater threat.

"You need to leave, son."

"I'm not leaving without her."

I don't hear Scott approach, but Dax does. As Scott's fingers wrap around my upper arm, Dax spins again. This time, as he shifts me around, his arm whips out and his fingers wrap around Scott's throat.

Scott releases me, and I stagger back. Dax stands there. Arm outstretched. Fingers wrapped around Scott's throat. Scott's face turns ruddy. He grasps at Dax's fingers and gulps for air.

Knowing enough to not get in Dax's way, I do the only thing which makes sense. I place myself between my father, his shotgun, and the man I love.

Dax says nothing, but I feel the lethality of his glare. It reflects off Scott's wide, terrified eyes. In the blink of an eye, Dax's powerful muscles bunch, then release in a fury. His fist makes contact with Scott's jaw while his iron grip releases its hold on Scott's throat.

Scott crumples.

It's the only way I can describe it.

Scott's entire body drops to the ground and he doesn't move.

Dax kneels beside Scott and feels for a pulse at his neck. He glances up at me, darkness brewing in his eyes, then his attention shifts to my father.

"He'll live." In one fluid movement, Dax is back on his feet. He takes my hand in his and marches out the door.

My father steps to the side, mouth agape, shock filling his face. His mouth moves, but no words come out.

Dax gives a high-pitched whistle and, seconds later, Dynamo runs toward him.

"I'm taking you out of here." He pulls me to him and drapes an arm over my shoulder.

At his truck, he opens the passenger door. Dynamo jumps inside and hops into the back seat. Dax helps me up, then glances over his shoulder at the silhouette of my father standing in the doorway.

He shuts the door, sealing me inside, then walks around the front of his truck. The entire time, his attention stays on my father and his gun.

Before I know it, the truck's in gear. Dirt and gravel spin out from beneath the tires, and we head down the lane.

Now that I have a minute to think, I clutch my midsection. My stomach squeezes and I feel like I'm going to be sick. Did that just happen? Did Dax just take Scott out? He defied my father.

"Where are we going?"

"I'm taking you home." Dax reaches over and grips my thigh. "I know things look bad right now, but you need to know everything is going to be okay."

I don't know how that's possible, but if anyone can deliver on that promise it'll be Dax.

"And where is that?"

"Texas."

TWENTY-ONE

Dax

———

I KEEP MY COMMENTS SHORT. RAGE BURNS IN MY VEINS AND THAT isn't something Dani needs to see. Hell, she's already seen too much of what I'm capable of, what I can do. It took all of my restraint not to kill Scott.

Her father made a deal with the devil and doesn't realize what he did. I don't know what kind of financial trouble the ranch might, or might not be in, but I know a thing or two about mineral rights. Studer must be sitting on millions, but that doesn't explain why he bartered his daughter's happiness away.

I'm well versed in all the shady practices people are capable of when they think they can take advantage of someone. If Studer has money problems, some of this messed up situation makes sense, but there's no way Studer would give up millions if he knew what his land was really worth.

It's the first thing I intend to look into. If there are reports of the land filed, it won't take much to figure things out.

"What exactly did I walk into there?" Maybe Dani can confirm my suspicions.

She rubs at her arms and keeps twisting around to look back the way we came.

"I think…maybe…you should take me back," she says.

"There's no way in hell I'm taking you back there. At least, not until I understand what was going on."

She draws in a deep breath. "It's all a mess."

"It looked fucked up. Has he ever hurt you before?"

I catch her covering four red marks on her arm. Four marks for four fingers I want to break.

"No. That was the first time."

"It wouldn't have been the last."

"Scott's never done that before."

"He did it one too many times. A man who cheats on a woman, and then puts marks on her, is dangerous. How about you tell me what was going on?"

She worries her lower lip and continues tossing glances over her right shoulder.

"I really think I need to go back."

"You're not going back."

"Don't tell me what to do." A warning tone vibrates in her voice.

"Dani…"

"Stop the car." Her screech cuts through the tenseness of the cab, and slices right into my heart.

Without thinking, I slam on the breaks and pull over on the shoulder. I lift my hands off the steering wheel and hold them up in surrender.

"Fair's fair, but let me tell you how I read this situation."

She gives a huff and places her hand on the door handle. When it looks like she's about to jump out of the truck and walk back to the ranch, I force myself to be calm. After what I saw in her house, the last thing I need to be doing is force her to do anything she doesn't want to do. But, I'll do everything in my power to get her to see reason.

She glances at me and her lower lip trembles.

"I'm tired of people I trust telling me what to do. Don't do that to me, Dax."

"Fine. Let me say what I need to say, and if you want to go home afterwards, I'll take you back."

"You promise?"

"Promise."

"Fine."

I lead with a question.

"You going to tell me what I walked into back there?"

I'm still not certain I understand everything.

"You're the great reader of the *situation*." Her tone gets snippy. "What do you think?"

"Fine, you want to play it that way, we'll play, but remember I'm on your side."

When it doesn't look like she's going to jump in and explain what was going on, I let out my breath and do my best to connect the dots.

"I don't know everything, but I can guess a few things. Your father is in debt and whatever it is, it's bad enough for him to make an arrangement with that asshole that involves you. I'm also guessing your father is being taking advantage of by Scott, which is something I intend to verify. If you think the best thing for you right now is to hop back into that shit-storm, then I'll turn around and take you home. If, however, you're as smart as I think you are, and if you're feeling any bit of what I'm feeling, then I'm hoping you'll consider another option."

"What option is that?"

"Come home with me."

"I can't leave. I need to make sure my father's okay."

"What do you know about whatever arrangement he made with Scott?"

"Not much, except it has to do with mineral rights and tying the knot with me." She shudders and looks like she's going to be sick.

I feel the same.

"That's what I figured. Now, we'll sort everything out, but I can't stay." Not now. I made a promise to my mother I need to keep, and if the worst happens, I need to see my father one last time. "I have a jet picking me up in Bozeman and I'm hoping you'll be on it with me."

"I can't." The snippiness in her voice turns to honest disappointment. I feel it deep in my bones. She *wants* to come with me, but is torn by her duty to her father.

"Why not?"

"First of all, I don't have the money for a ticket."

I can't help the smirk which lands on my face. Dani is in for a big shock.

She misunderstands my expression, because she continues. "And I don't care what you say, you're not buying me one. I don't borrow from boyfriends."

"Well, at least we sorted that out."

"What's that?"

"My status. Although I'm considering something much more permanent than *boyfriend.*"

"Cocky much?" The grin lifting the corners of her lips makes my heart lift for joy. I'm breaking through her anger.

"You haven't seen anything yet. Now, how about we discuss Texas."

"I don't think you're listening."

"Hun, I listened to every word. You don't need to buy a ticket, and I'm not buying one for you. You weren't *listening* to me. I said I have a jet picking me up. I never said I was flying commercial."

Her brows draw tight together. "You have a jet?"

"Actually, my family owns a few jets, but only one flew up to get me." I reach for her hand. "I really need to get home. Something happened to my father."

There must be a hitch in my voice because she suddenly lunges at me and wraps her arms around me, trying to offer me comfort.

"Oh, Dax!" All she accomplishes is getting me hard in under three-seconds flat.

I laugh and shift her around, settling her on my lap. That may not be the best move, because once she's in my arms I don't want to let her go. She wiggles, rubbing her ass over my growing erection.

"You should stop that unless you want me to fuck you right here." My warning comes with a low growl.

She glances down the darkened highway. We haven't seen a single car since we left the ranch.

"How about you tell me how a drifter cowboy has a jet picking him up?" She wiggles again, this time with seductive invitation. "And I'll decide whether to relieve your...um...discomfort."

"My discomfort? Having problems with your words again?"

Her face flushes and she refuses to meet my eyes. I try to get her to look at me. For some reason, I have an irrational urge to hear her say the word *cock*. Or *dick*. Hell, at this point I want her mouth on my dick, because the pressure is building and the more she squirms the harder I get.

"My words are perfectly fine, and appropriate for a lady."

I tug her tight. "Be a lady in public. With me, I want all the filthy words and your darkest pleasures."

She pokes me in the chest. "I thought you needed to catch a plane."

"It's a jet, not a plane, and yes…" I vent a deep sigh. "We do need to get going."

"I'm sorry about your dad. What happened?"

"I don't know. My mother was vague on the phone. She doesn't understand medical stuff. All I know is that he's in the ICU."

She practically hops off my lap. "Shit Dax! Why didn't you say something? We need to go."

I make a point to reach down and adjust my erection. "You have a way of distracting me." A quick debate in my head occurs, wondering if I should take her in the truck and relieve the pressure, or do exactly as she says. At least one thing is settled. Dani is coming with me.

Unwilling to press my luck, I put the truck in gear and head back down the highway. Bozeman is still some distance away.

In the darkness, silence descends between us. I enjoy these moments as much or more than our banter. I've never really been the kind of person who enjoys silence, and it often makes me uncomfortable. With Dani, I don't need to be anything special, or struggle to impress her. It's relaxing to simply exist.

Dynamo whines a few miles down the road and I pull off at an intersection.

"Sorry, 'Mo needs to stretch his legs and pee."

Dani climbs out of the truck and joins me on the side of the road. We stand shoulder to shoulder, not quite touching, as Dynamo pees on every bush in sight. Off in the distance the lowing of cows rolls through the still air. Crickets chirp, and the wind rustles through the long grass.

"It's beautiful out here, isn't it?" Dani bumps my shoulder with hers.

I reach down, take her hand in mine, and bring her knuckles to my lips.

"Because you're here."

Moonlight glitters in her eyes as she stares up at me. Then her brows pinch together. "You never answered my question."

"Which question?"

"How you have a jet coming to pick you up."

"How much do you know about cattle?"

"Quite a bit considering I grew up on a ranch and I'm studying to be a large animal vet. I know pretty much everything."

"Okay, that might not have been the right question. How much do you know about the cattle industry?"

She shrugs. "I'm not really interested in the business side of things." A frown pulls at the corners of her lips, tipping her gentle smile upside down. "I guess I should have paid more attention. If I had, then my dad..."

I squeeze her hand. "I don't want you to worry about your dad. I have thoughts about what we can do."

"We?" Her shoulders hunch. "I'm afraid I'm the whole reason he's in this mess. He financed my education. Eight years of school is a minor fortune." A gasp escapes her and she squeezes my hand. "What am I going to do about next year?"

She releases my hand and stabs her fingers into her hair. Dynamo trots back, then stops suddenly to take a dump not ten feet from us.

"'Mo! Really?" I grab Dani's arm and spin her around while Dynamo drops his load. "Dani," I try to get her attention, but she isn't listening.

Sensitive to what happened earlier, I give her the slightest of shakes, just enough to get her to look at me, and hopefully not enough to remind her of the brutality of that asshole Scott.

She wipes at her cheeks and does the most amazing thing. Instead of pulling away, she throws herself into my embrace. Her tiny form fits perfectly in my arms and the top of her head tucks nicely under my chin.

"I don't know if I can finish school. I don't want to drop out, but now..."

I run my fingers through the long length of her hair.

"I'm going to take care of you. I'll pay for the rest of your school."

"I can't accept that."

I grip her arms and hold her away from me. It's the only way to duck down and get eye level with her. She needs to hear what I have to say.

"I take care of what's mine, Dani. Do you hear me? You're the one I want, and I want all your dreams to come true."

"I don't feel right taking money from you."

"You mean from us."

Her brows scrunch with confusion.

"Everything I have is yours."

"I..."

"Don't argue with me. Where I come from, that's usually how it works in a marriage."

It may not be the best proposal in the world, but I don't regret it. Not having Dani by my side for the rest of my life makes no sense. In my mind, being married to her is a foregone conclusion.

"We're not married." Her voice is so soft, I strain to hear.

"But we will be."

"Is this a proposal?"

"I guess so."

"You need to step up your game, because that's the worst proposal ever."

"You don't like it?"

"No." She ticks points off with her fingers. "First off, you're not even on one knee. Second, there's no ring. Third, and this is the most important part, you don't have my father's blessing."

"Is that all?"

"Isn't it enough?"

"You didn't answer me."

"I don't think you actually asked." She crosses her arms over her chest and tries to give me a stern look, but she can't hold the fierceness that requires and winds up giggling instead.

Dynamo finishes his business and heads for the truck.

"Well, considering you didn't say *Hell no!* I'm calling it a win. It's a done deal, Miss Dani Studer, or rather the future Mrs. Dani Kingston."

She stumbles backwards. "Kingston? As in Kingston Ranch, the largest ranch in the United States?"

I shrug. "Yeah, guess I should have said something sooner."

She punches me in the arm. "Seriously!" She makes air quotes. "*I know a little about ranching.* Shit, Dax, my father is going to piss himself. You're rancher royalty. Home to over tens of thousands of cattle with holdings of nearly a million...*a Million!*...acres. And you've been hanging out on Crowbar Ranch during calving season?" She gathers her hair and pulls it over her shoulder. Her fingers absently thread through her hair, dividing it, and weaving it into one of the sloppiest braids I've ever seen.

"I guess so."

"What are you doing here? Why aren't you helping out at home?"

My cell phone buzzes.

"The jet landed." I scratch my head. "Do you mind finishing this rather enlightening conversation on the way *to* Texas? I kind of need to get home."

She releases her hair and the strands unwind. "Shit. Your father. I'm so sorry. I'm rattling on and on while he's..." She lifts a finger and shakes it at me. "This conversation is not over."

"Of course not. We have the rest of our lives to finish it, my future wife."

"I have not said yes." She stomps her foot.

"No, but you will." I laugh at her indignant *huff* and climb inside the truck. Dynamo is already curled into a ball and opens a lazy eye as if wondering when we'll get the show on the road. I kind of wonder the same thing, and it occurs to me if I should give my mother a heads up that she'll soon be meeting her future daughter-in-law.

TWENTY-TWO

Dani

_____

Kingston Ranch?

I shake my head with disbelief as we drive into the Bozeman Yellowstone International Airport. Instead of parking in the parking area, next to the terminal, Dax heads to the industrial side of the airport.

"Where are we going?"

"Private jets don't use the commercial terminal," he says.

Since he seems to know what he's doing, I sit back and exchange a look with Dynamo. Strangely, my biggest fear isn't about my family losing everything, but losing the man I've come to love.

Is the jet-setting Dax the same man who rescued me from the bluff? The same Dax who held me in his arms on horseback? The one who slept beneath the stars because he doesn't like being close to too many people?

Do I know him at all?

The first, and most immediate answer, is unequivocally, yes.

That does nothing to stop my doubts. The man who parks outside the small private terminal walks with casual grace, like he's done this a thousand times. His family owns jets, plural.

I'm still wrapping my head around that.

And they own the largest cattle operation in the country, maybe the world. What the hell brought him to the tiny town of Bear Springs and Crowbar Ranch?

My mouth gapes the entire time as he holds my hand and draws me into the private terminal. Airport security amounts to stepping through a metal detector. There's none of the highly invasive full body scans that reveal everything to some nameless person behind a screen. I don't have to kick off my shoes, remove my jacket, or place my laptop in a bin.

Dynamo explores every nook and cranny of the place. No leash. No crate. Just a dog running amok. It feels surreal. Not that Dynamo misbehaves. He's the most attentive and smartest dog I've ever known. He triggers off Dax, constantly checking in with his master for the next command. For now, Dax lets the dog explore.

Dax places his wallet on a conveyer belt to be x-rayed when I realize I have no form of identification. My departure from my house was abrupt, and that's putting it lightly. There was no time to grab a purse, pack clothes, or grab a toothbrush. I basically have nothing other than the clothes on my back.

"Um, Dax?" I halt at a small grouping of plush chairs. There are no uncomfortable rows of plastic seats crammed into a crowded waiting area. This is a space designed for those accustomed to the finer things in life. I expect a waiter to appear at any moment and offer us champagne.

"What's up?"

"I don't have my purse. No ID. I can't get on that plane."

He tugs me to his chest. "You don't need any of that."

"I'm pretty sure I need ID to get on a plane." I almost say I need a ticket, but stop at the last minute. I'm fairly certain tickets are not required, but there must be some kind of passenger manifest?

"Only when you're flying commercial, but not for a private jet."

"But I don't have a change of clothes." I feel myself digging in my heels. There's something intimidating about climbing onboard his jet, as if a veil is lifting and I'm seeing a whole new person.

My Dax is gone and that terrifies me. It might be better to run home and face whatever plans Scott has for me than watch the man I love transform into a stranger.

"We'll take care of that." Again, he gives reassurance.

And he uses that word again, *We*, like it's a foregone conclusion I accepted his very lame proposal. His money isn't my money, and I don't accept charity from others.

"I don't have a toothbrush." I'm running out of excuses.

Dynamo returns and nuzzles my palm. Maybe he senses some of my distress, because Dax isn't listening. What he does is sweep me off my feet, silencing my outburst with a kiss meant for the movies. It even comes with the requisite dip.

I love the little flutter in my belly and that solid sense of rightness beating in my chest. This is the Dax I remember.

"I don't have a toothbrush either, but we'll make do. You promised to trust me."

Actually, I don't remember that. But I do trust him. Dax will take care of me. Maybe that's what scares me the most. My father didn't raise me to need a man to take care of me. I don't mind choosing to let a man help out, but *need?*

That feels wrong.

A man in a pilot's uniform enters through a set of glass double doors. When the doors slide open the roar of jet engines rolls in with him.

"Nice to see you, Dax." He greets Dax with a firm handshake. The name on his shirt says Logan Reid.

"You too. Thanks for coming to get me."

"Anytime." The pilot's attention shifts to me. "I was only expecting one passenger."

"This is Dani Studer. She's coming with us."

"Nice to meet you, Miss Studer." Logan extends his hand and I return a hesitant shake.

"Likewise."

The pilot turns back to Dax. "If you're ready to go, we can leave any time."

"We're ready." Dax follows the pilot out the double doors, dragging me behind him with a gentle tug. It's the warmth in his eyes, however, which moves my feet. This man loves me. I see it. Feel it. And know it with all my heart.

I think to argue one more time about why I can't go, but snap my mouth shut when I see the jet he leads me toward. I expect something small, not a plane with one, two…ten windows along the fuselage? How big is this thing?

Promising myself I'm not going to look like a country hick and stare, I struggle to retain my cool. Then promptly lose it when I stumble at the top of the stairs.

There aren't regular airplane seats inside. Instead, groupings of leather covered recliners fill the interior, along with a couch. Luxurious doesn't even come close.

Dax grins and leads me to two of the recliners in the back which face each other.

"I like sitting in the back," he says. "It's more private."

The pilot disappears into the cockpit, leaving us alone. Dynamo sniffs at all the leather and cocks his head at Dax.

Dax pats a seat cushion. "Up here boy."

Dynamo jumps into the overstuffed recliner and circles around until settling down. Dax doesn't seem concerned about Dynamo's claws scuffing the expensive leather.

"This belongs to your family?"

He gives a sheepish nod. "Yeah."

"Okay, let's just say I was interested to know which of your family's jets this was. Is this the big jet or the little jet?"

He laughs. "I thought we discussed that size doesn't matter?"

"Says the man with an impressively well-endowed cock."

He presses his hands to his cheeks in mock surprise. "Did you just use a filthy word? My sweet girl?" He lowers his hands and shakes his head side to side. "I'm not sure what I'm going to do with you."

There's no one else on the plane. I can't help but tease Dax.

"Well, I can think of one or two things." I make a show of licking my lips. "I have a confession to make."

"You do?"

"And it may change everything."

"Is that so?"

I step toward him and drag my fingers down his chest. The fabric of his shirt bunches together at his waist. I lift on tiptoe and whisper into his ear. "I'm not a member of the mile-high club. I don't think I can fly with you. You'll have to take me back."

His deep laugh reverberates inside the cabin. "I'm certain we can do something about that."

The pilot opens the door to the front cabin and looks over his shoulder. "We're ready to go. Do all the sitting in the seat stuff, buckling up the seat belts, locking the trays in their full and upright position. You know the drill."

I glance around. There isn't one tray in sight. Looks like our pilot has a sense of humor.

"That's our cue." Dax gestures to one of the chairs. "Buckle up babe."

"As you wish." I settle in the seat opposite him and strap in. Even the belt buckles radiate luxury. I glance around the cabin. "What, no flight attendants?"

"Yeah, this is the economy flight. No frills."

"I'm teasing."

"I know, but I don't think my mother was thinking about ancillary crew when she told Logan to fetch her son."

His comment gives me pause because it reminds me why Dax needs to get home. I reach for his hand.

"I hope he's all right."

"Me too." He gives my hand a squeeze then takes his seat.

We spend the flight in relative silence. Despite my comment about the mile-high club, Dax grows more introspective. His brow furrows when he thinks I'm not looking, although he always puts on a smile when our eyes meet. Dynamo crawls out of his chair to sit at Dax's feet, providing a kind of comfort I can't.

There will be plenty of time for fooling around later, and it's probably for the best we don't force sex during the flight. He has a lot on his mind and spends the majority of his time texting on his phone. The plane must have wi-fi, not that I'd know. I don't have my phone, which makes me worry for my father.

He doesn't know where I am, what I'm doing, only that Dax yanked me out the front door and disappeared with me into the night. That was several hours ago. By now, my father is probably beside himself with worry. It occurs to me to ask Dax to borrow his phone, but from the way he cups it in his hands and the worry lines creasing his face, I can wait.

After a quick search, I find a book hidden in one of the compartments between the seats, a historical romance about cowboys. It keeps me grinning with some of the outlandish situations the couple find themselves in, but more importantly, it passes the time.

Before long, the pilot announces we're landing. Smooth as silk, Logan brings us to the ground and taxies to the terminal. With a glance out the window, I'm not the least surprised by the black SUV waiting for us.

Dynamo perks up his ears, stretches, and wags his tail. I agree with him. I'm ready to get off the plane too. Not really sure of Dax's state of mind, I take my lead from him. He unbuckles and draws me to him, tugging me tight against his broad chest. He takes in a deep breath, burying his nose in the soft angle of my neck.

"Sorry I ignored you during the flight. I was talking with my mother."

"How is she holding up?"

"She's stressed. My father had a heart attack. He has near total occlusion of his LAD."

As a veterinary student I understand his concern. One of the main coronary arteries which supplies blood to the heart, the left anterior descending artery is often called the widow maker. If the blood through the artery becomes one hundred percent blocked, it's almost always fatal without emergency care.

I place my hand on his arm, providing what comfort I can. "How is your father?"

From the grief on Dax's face, I can't tell if his father is still alive or passed during the flight. Dax can be incredibly stoic and I feel lost in how to comfort him.

"They took him to emergency surgery. The LAD is 99% occluded and he had blockages in his other coronary arteries. They're doing a quadruple bypass."

"We need to get there, Dax."

He takes both my hands in his. "Yes, *we* do. If my father makes it through surgery, I want to introduce him to his future daughter-in-law. I know this isn't exactly the best meet-the-parents scenario, but I'm really glad you're here."

I cup his jaw. "I wouldn't have it any other way." And in my heart, I know that for the truth it is. He may not have knocked my socks off with a fancy proposal, but there's no doubt he's the one I want, forever and always, we are one.

Logan cracks open the outer hatch and lowers the stairs.

"You can deplane now."

Dax heads for the exit, Dynamo is right beside him. Dax stops at the door and gives Logan a shake. "Thanks for the ride."

"Anytime." As I exit, Logan tips an imaginary hat at me. "Nice meeting you, Miss Studer."

"Nice meeting you too."

"Take care of him," Logan says, "he's a good man."

I don't understand the relationship between Dax and Logan, but there seems to be a friendship between them deeper than that of employer and employee.

"I will." And with that said, I step out of the plane and into the unknown.

This is Dax's world. It's much bigger than my tiny town of Bear Creek. Whatever happens, I vow to remember the man who sleeps beneath the stars.

TWENTY-THREE

Dax

I FEEL BAD IGNORING DANI DURING MOST OF THE FLIGHT, BUT MY mother's texts keep me on edge. I spend most of my time trying to calm her down, knowing how lost she must feel all by herself at the hospital.

My mother doesn't understand the nuances of medical terminology, and doctors often fail to explain in layman terms, not realizing the terror the unknown causes in loved ones who don't understand what's going on.

I try to piece together what my mother knows, what she understands, and then try to use my medical training to break everything down, using language she can understand.

When she said my father's coronaries are completely blocked, I feared for the worst, but gentle questioning gives me the knowledge I need to maintain hope and lend what strength I can from thirty-thousand feet in the air.

And I feel bad for Dani. She clings to my side, sticking closer than Dynamo, and keeps secreting worried glances at me. I want to tell her not to worry, but her concern isn't for my father. It's for me, and I don't know how I feel about the whole situation.

She sits beside me and interlaces her fingers with mine. Without a word, she leans her head against my shoulder. It's late and she must be tired. With my father's condition, I haven't given enough consideration to what she's going through with her father and that asshole, Scott.

"How are you holding up?" I bump her chin softly with my knuckles.

A yawn escapes her. "A bit tired, but otherwise okay."

"Do you want me to take you to the hotel?" I was going to head straight to the hospital. My mother needs me by her side, but Dani looks beat.

She traces the lines on my palm. "I want to be with you, at least if you want me there. Or, you can take me to the hotel and go by yourself?"

"I want you with me." I kiss the top of her head. "We'll figure out what to do about your father, Dani. I promise."

"My father can wait…" She doesn't finish the sentence, but I feel the subtext like a stab to the gut.

I have no idea how much time my father has, or even if he'll be alive when we arrive.

"You're amazing, you know that?" I run my fingers through her hair, loving the way the silken locks feel against my skin.

"You're not too bad yourself."

Dynamo whines beside me and I lean forward to speak with the driver. "Do you mind stopping somewhere where I can walk my dog?" Hell, what am I going to do with Dynamo? Hospitals don't allow dogs, unless they're service animals, and I never got around to filing the paperwork.

I sort that out with a quick trip to a pet store and make arrangements with the driver. When the driver drops us off at the hospital, I know Dynamo will be in good hands. Already, the dog jumps into the front passenger seat, tongue out, and presses his nose against the glass. I dismiss the driver until later and head inside with my future bride by my side.

Finding where to go isn't difficult. A quick stop for directions at the information counter, where we're provided visitor badges, and we're off to the elevators.

"Does your mother know I'm with you?" Dani shifts from foot to foot and her grip on my hand tightens.

I can imagine the stress meeting my mother must put on Dani. It was different for me. I met her father first.

"She doesn't, but don't worry. My mother is a saint, very open-hearted, and welcoming."

"She may not want a stranger in the middle of a family emergency."

"Once she sees you, you won't be a stranger. Relax."

"Easy for you to say," she says with a grump, but I can tell she doesn't mean it.

The doors to the elevator open, dumping us at the PACU waiting room. My mother automatically looks up. It takes half a second before it hits that her son has arrived. Ever the one for proper decorum, she puts her book down first, takes notice of Dani, then stands and smoothes out the wrinkles of her dress.

She doesn't rush, or scream, or make a scene. There's no other way to describe it other than to say Elizabeth Kingston glides across the room with a serene smile fixed on her beautiful face.

Dani mentioned rancher royalty and is closer to the mark than she realizes. Elizabeth Kingston reigns over local society. The Kingston name carries weight in Texas.

"You made it." My mother places her hand on my arm. Not one for public displays of affection, she holds herself with poise and class, but I see the cracks in her façade. My mother is falling apart from the inside out.

I ignore her attempt at being discreet and pull my mother in for a hug. I see the pain in her eyes, the worry, the fear, and her stoic resolve to weather whatever comes next. For a moment, I hold my mother and give her the shoulder she needs to cry on.

The moment my arms wrap around her slender form, the tension in her body melts away. She presses her cheek to my chest and gives the tiniest sniffle. It'll be the only public display of emotion she'll give.

Dani steps to the side, giving the two of us as much privacy as she can in the busy waiting room.

"How is he?" I ask.

My mother pulls away and forces a smile. Ever so discreetly, she wipes at her cheek.

"He's in surgery. They couldn't wait."

"I wouldn't expected them to. Have you heard anything?"

She shakes her head. Rather than discussing my father any further, my mother turns her attention to Dani.

"Who is your guest?" Her eyes flick between us, taking note of the tiniest nuance of Dani's body language.

I don't hesitate. "Mother, this is Dani Studer. Dani, this is my mother, Elizabeth Kingston."

"It's very nice to meet you." My mother gives Dani a welcoming hug, kissing both her cheeks without actually pressing lips to skin. It's cordial, polite, and proper, yet cautiously distant.

"It's a pleasure to meet you, Mrs. Kingston, but I wish it wasn't under these circumstances. I hope for a full recovery for your husband."

"Thank you, dear, that is very kind." My mother's gaze flicks down to Dani's empty ring finger and her brows draw together with confusion.

I rarely bring girl's home, and never in the midst of a family crisis. Since she suspects, I'm not going to keep her in suspense.

"Dani has agreed to marry me."

Dani stiffens beside me, but I don't blame her. I didn't discuss breaking the news to my parents. Not that she should be surprised.

"Is this true?" My mother's sadness slips away, replaced by joy. There's no hesitation either, no comments about how new our relationship must be. I love how she doesn't ask me, but rather turns to Dani for the answer. *Way to put my girl on the spot, mom.* But Dani handles it like a champ.

"Your son likes to think so, but he's yet to ask my father's permission and doesn't seem to know how to get on one knee." She lifts her left hand and points to her ring finger. "And as you can see, there is something sorely lacking. Has Dax always been a rule breaker? Making assumptions like this?"

My mother's smile brightens. "As a matter of fact, he's well known for leaping before he looks. Now, let's sit and have a chat. I want to hear about how you two met." She pulls Dani to where she was sitting, completely ignoring me. The two of them talk as if they've known each other forever.

A sigh of relief escapes me, although I don't know why I was nervous. Dani's amazing, a breath of fresh air, and perfect in every way. Of course she hits it off with my mother.

While the two of them talk, I head to the nurse's station to inquire about my father. The pretty receptionist says my father is still in surgery and to please have a seat. I return to my mother and Dani.

"How are you doing?" I drape an arm around Dani's shoulders.

Dani smiles. "I'm learning all your secrets."

Over the next hour, I sit there while my mother brings up every embarrassing memory of my life, most of them documented in the photos on her phone. Dani and my mother pass the time laughing over stories and pictures of my less than stellar life moments.

Finally, a man and woman approach dressed in surgical gear.

"Mrs. Kingston?" The woman asks.

"Yes?" My mother stands. Her voice shakes and her hands tremble. I leap to my feet, taking her hand in mine. Whatever the doctors have to say, I'll stand by my mother's side.

"Your husband is out of surgery." The female doctor smiles. "He's stable and in recovery."

My mother staggers against me, overcome. "Thank you." She barely gets the words out, before burying her face against my chest. A loud sob escapes her and I step up, asking the questions she can't.

"When can we see him?"

"Once the anesthesia wears off, he'll be able to accept visitors." The woman briefly explains the quadruple bypass, but is quick to reassure me that my father tolerated the procedure well. "He's not out of the woods. The next 24-72 hours will be critical and he'll need to stay in intensive care. After that, depending on how he does, we can move him to a monitored step-down unit."

"Thank you." I shake hands with both doctors and settle my mother back in her seat.

"How about I get coffee for everyone?" Dani looks between the two of us. "Mrs. Kingston is there any special way you like your coffee?"

It's going to be a long night. I appreciate Dani's gesture.

"Black with a little cream and sugar. Thank you, Dani, and please, call me Elizabeth."

"I'll be back in a bit." Dani excuses herself, maybe realizing we need a moment alone, but then she gestures for me to join her.

"What's up?"

"I don't have my purse." She bites at her lower lip. "Can I borrow some money?"

"You'll soon realize what's mine is yours. No need to ask."

She lifts her ring finger. "I'll ask until there's a ring here."

I shake my head. "You're not letting me live that down, are you?"

"You mean the world's worst proposal?"

I reach into my pocket and give her a credit card. "Get us something to eat while you're at it." When she reaches for the card, I yank it away. "I need a kiss first."

"A kiss? Your mother is watching us."

"I promise to keep my hands to myself."

"You sure you can keep that promise?"

A low chuckle escapes me, because I have every intention of squeezing her ass. I don't answer. Instead, I wrap an arm around her waist and pull her to me. Leaning down, I kiss her. It isn't passionate, but neither is it chaste. And, yes, I palm her ass, lifting her against me with a groan.

I selfishly wish we were by the riverside, staring up at the stars with a blazing fire and the soft lowing of cattle rumbling over the hills. I miss the simpleness of Bear Creek.

With my kiss delivered, I give Dani a light swat on the ass as the elevator doors ding open. She waves as they close, leaving me to return to my mother.

From the way my mother picks at the nonexistent lint on her dress, it's time to provide a little reassurance.

"How are you holding up?"

"I'm good." She isn't, but it's the proper thing to say.

"He's going to be all right." I try to inject as much confidence into my tone as possible.

"Thank you for coming." She leans against me. "I know the two of you have had your issues. It'll mean a lot to him that you're here."

"I know."

"Dani seems nice."

"She's amazing." At the mention of her name, warmth fills my chest.

"And she seems to have stolen my son's heart."

"She did."

"Is she the one?"

"Yes." It feels good saying it.

"Have you thought about a ring?"

"I was hoping to ask about grandma's ring."

"That's what I was going to suggest. Tell me about Dani."

I proceed to tell her how we met, about the feisty girl by the side of the road who gave me grief, about how I waited to make sure she finished changing the tire and was safe, and how I followed her to the diner.

"Bear Creek sounds like a wonderful town."

"It is."

"How did you ever wind up there?"

"Well, I got a dog."

"A dog?"

I mention the shelter and how it felt like fate to find Dynamo there. "I wasn't ready to come home. I lost so much when the Air Force boarded me out. I know father wants me home, but I needed to figure out what I wanted. Dynamo and I took to the road. I'd ask him left or right, and wound up in Montana."

"Your father loves you. I know he can be strict, and he expects so much from you. Don't fault him for wanting the best for you."

"Well, I didn't go far."

"Montana seems rather far."

"I mean, I got a job at Dani's father's ranch, helping out during calving season. Ranching is more in my blood than I thought."

"I guess so." My mother gives a secretive smile. "Does Dani know about Kingston Ranch?"

"She does now."

"You barely know her. Are you sure about marriage?"

"From the moment I met her, I've felt something I can't describe. She lights up my life. Breathing is easier around her. And when I'm with her I don't think about the things I've lost. All I can think about are the things I want to do with her." I pause and think about Dani, about how incredible she is, and I want my mother to feel it too. "She's in vet school."

"Is that so?"

"Yeah, has only a year to go." I purse my lips wondering how hard Dani will fight me when I tell her I'll be paying for the rest of her education.

"I sense something you're not saying."

My mother is perceptive. I tell her about the crazy deal Dani's father arranged with Scott and his family.

"We've had our run-ins with those sorts," she says with a nod. "Tell me what you're thinking?"

"I'm thinking I need to put a ring on her finger fast, and I need to fix things with her father. I basically abducted her."

"Dani doesn't look like a kidnap victim."

"She's not, but we still have to sort out what to do about her father. Crowbar Ranch would be a great addition to the Kingston brand."

"Ah, I was wondering how you were going to fix that. It can work. Costly though to annex a ranch out of state."

"Yeah, I don't think father will support it, but I have enough on my own to make it work. I'm not walking away from this."

"I wouldn't expect you to, but don't write off your father just yet. He's going to need your help to run Kingston Ranch after this. I hope you'll consider coming home. The two of you need to learn to work together and it's time for you to take over control of the business. How is that going to work with Dani? Have you thought about that? Where will the two of you live? Bear Creek? Or here?"

"I don't know, but I have a year to figure that out."

"I'm sure you'll do the right thing."

Twenty minutes later, one of the nurses from intensive care approaches us. "Mrs. Kingston?"

"Yes?"

"Your husband is awake and asking for you."

"Come, let's go." My mother stands.

"Only one visitor at a time in post op recovery." The nurse gives an apologetic look. "I'm sorry."

"You go, hun." My mother gestures for me to go with the nurse. "Your father will be happy to see you."

"You go. I'll wait."

Dani has yet to return with the coffee and I want to be here when she does. Although from the way she and my mother seem to hit things off, maybe I don't need to worry.

"You should go." She tries to insist. "It'll do him good to see you."

"I'll see him, but a man needs to see his wife after something like this. I'm good, mother, another few minutes won't matter. Go to him."

She brushes at wetness on her cheeks and follows the nurse back behind the double doors marked PACU, leaving me to wait alone.

I rub my palms against my jeans, nervous to see my father. Seth Kingston is intimidating on the best of days. I don't know what kind of state I'll find my father in, but brace for the worst.

TWENTY-FOUR

Dax

———

A FEW MINUTES LATER, A DIFFERENT NURSE RETURNS AND approaches me.

"Mr. Kingston?"

I look up. "Yes?"

"You may go back now."

"I thought there was only one visitor at a time?"

"Your father can be quite persuasive."

"Are you sure it's okay? Is my father…"

"Your father is recovering quickly. He's going to keep all of us on our toes." From her frazzled look, I figure that's an apt statement. I glance at the elevator. Dani has yet to return with the coffee. "I'm expecting my fiancée to return with coffee. I don't want her to think I ran off."

The nurse inclines her head. "Don't worry, Mr. Kingston. We're used to this. Let's tell the people at the front desk and they'll keep an eye out. She'll be fine. Your father…" She shakes her head.

I hold back a grin. I know how tenacious my father can be.

"You would make my day if we didn't keep him waiting." She twists her fingers and I see the effort she makes to remain professional.

"Done deal. I know exactly what you're talking about." I brace myself as much as possible, but I'm not prepared for the frail looking man hooked up to monitoring equipment in the PACU.

"Alexander…" My father's greeting is more of a croak than a robust shout.

I approach and grip my father's shaky hand.

"Father, you look…" Weak? Frail? Nearly dead?

"I look like shit. It's been a rough go, but I'm not dead yet."

"No sir, you are not." I don't appreciate my father's humor, and from the expression on my mother's face, she doesn't either.

"Well, I don't plan on leaving just yet. You and I have some things to discuss. First off, you need to come home. Kingston Ranch needs you."

I give my mother a look, telling her I'll try my best to behave, but that I'll likely fail.

"Honey," she soothes, stroking Seth Kingston's hair back from his face, "you said you would behave."

"Do you see this?" My father gestures to my mom. "Already, she's treating me like a child. I'm not an invalid."

"I never said you were, and Seth Kingston, you promised."

"Oh, all right." My father says with a grumble.

Not one to step in-between my parent's arguments, or whatever this is, I do just that.

"She's treating you like a man who should be resting but is already running the nursing staff ragged. You need to take it easy."

"I don't know what that means. Speaking of, your mother says you have news and a business proposition."

"Wow, mother, I thought maybe you'd let me tell him." Not that I'm surprised. My parents share everything.

"I'm simply running interference for two blockheads." She rubs my father's hand, stroking the pale flesh. Her lower lip trembles, but her voice comes out strong enough.

"Blockhead? Is that the best you can come up with Beth?" My father gives an indignant snort.

"For now," she says, "and you promised…"

"Yes, yes, I know, and I'm a man of my word." He lifts a finger and points at me. "Your mother says you've found a girl, need my mama's ring, and want to swoop in and save the day by annexing her family's ranch."

"Father…" I grit my teeth.

The way my father says it makes the whole thing sound silly, as if I haven't thought through everything that can go wrong. Or, as if I haven't considered all the reasons Dani and I should slow things down.

None of it matters.

I'm marrying Dani, with or without my father's blessing. Something tells me all three of Dani's conditions need to be met before she'll officially say yes.

"Are you going to give me grandma's ring, or not?"

"That depends. Tell me about Crowbar Ranch. Convince me it's a good business proposition and the ring is yours."

I'm prepared to present a business plan to my father. I didn't waste my time on the flight down from Montana.

Twenty minutes later, I have my father's blessing, the promise of my grandmother's ring, and a proposition for Dani's father.

After our conversation, my father's complexion seems paler than before. I check the monitors. My experience as a paramedic comes to good use in times like these, but there's nothing worrisome in the readouts. In fact, my father's heart rate, blood pressure, and oxygen levels are all normal. Better than I expect, in fact.

I take a moment to really look at the man. Age isn't settling well on my father, weakening the strong man I've always admired, and feared.

After our talk, where my father listened rather than dominated the conversation, I fear him a little less and find new respect for my father's mind for business. Not once does he reject the idea of annexing Crowbar Ranch and folding it into Kingston properties.

He does raise some concerns and offers a different, novel solution to the problem. It's something unique and allows Dani's father to retain full control. A gentleman's agreement, it respects Studer's autonomy.

"I'm going to check on Dani."

"Do you want to meet her?" My mother fusses over my father.

"I would, but maybe not just yet. I'm feeling a little tired."

Tired? My father looks ten shades past exhausted.

"Mother, we should let father rest."

"Yes, of course, dear. I'll be out in a minute." She settles into a nearby chair.

I leave my parents to say goodbye and find Dani waiting for me with three steaming cups of coffee.

"Sorry to have left you."

She stands and wraps her arms around me. "Don't ever be sorry for taking care of your family. I'll wait as long as it takes."

"How long do you have?"

"What do you mean?"

"Before you have to get back to school. This is your Spring Break, isn't it?"

"We have a couple of days left."

"Good."

"What are you thinking?" She gives me a look like she doesn't trust me.

"I'm thinking I want to show you my home. Are you too tired for another flight?"

"As long as I'm with you? Never."

I like that answer. Now that I know my father isn't actively trying to die, a weight lifts off my shoulders. Which is funny considering my father basically gave over the entire operation of Kingston ranch and all its holdings to me.

"Let's get out of here." I whisper into her ear, nibbling her earlobe until a blush fills her face.

"What about your mother?"

"My mother won't be leaving my father's side. They'll have to pry her away."

I don't exactly say goodbye to my mother, but we exchange a look. My parents fell in love at first sight. She understands the feelings I have for the woman I intend to call my wife.

I lead Dani downstairs and a very excited Dynamo greets us in the SUV.

An hour later, we're in the air, heading west toward my home. I suddenly get the urge to lay Dani out on one of the leather couches and thoroughly kiss her senseless. Hell, who am I kidding? I ache to fuck her and stake my claim, not as a boyfriend, but rather as her One and Only.

Adrenaline rushes through me thinking about laying her out for my pleasure. It's mixed with more than a fair helping of awe. She wants me, as much or more than I want her. This thing between us feels right, like her heart belongs exclusively to me. Not for a fleeting second, but for an eternity.

I want to express physically what that means, all the emotions I feel but repress with my family emergency.

Finally, I can't contain myself any longer. There's only one problem. We're less than ten-minutes from landing.

"Excuse me a second."

Dani looks up from the book she's reading. She found it on our flight down to Texas and is nearly at the end. She reads fast.

"Okay." She buries her nose back in the book while I knock on the door to the cockpit.

"Come in."

I push on the door and poke my head inside. "How far out are we?"

"Should be starting our descent in just a few minutes. Why?" Logan's gaze flicks past me to Dani sitting in the back.

"Any way you can circle around for a bit?"

Logan winks. "You're the boss. Consider it done."

I retreat, making sure to shut the pilot's door. I sit beside Dani.

"How's the book?"

"Not too bad, considering." She holds up the trashy 80's romance novel.

I recognize it as one of my mother's favorites by the wear on the spine and the way the pages curl.

I trace a circle over Dani's thigh, starting just above her knee and moving inexorably up. "That went pretty well with my parents, didn't it?"

She puts the book down and her attention shifts to the progress of my hand. "It went very well. Your mother is amazing, and I'm really happy your father's surgery was a success."

"Yes, it was, but it's still going to be a long road to recovery. He needs me to help out at home."

"I kind of figured that. You're going to have to leave Bear Creek."

"Not for long, and it's not like you're going to be there anyway. Not when you return to school."

"True. I just need to steer clear of Scott and I might just make it to the end of the year."

"I want to talk about what comes next." I tap the cover of her book. "Our story will make a pretty good book, don't you think?"

"It would."

"I know how to make it happen." I tell her about my conversation with my father, needing to know if what we proposed might be of interest. "What do you think?"

"I think the next conversation you have with my dad shouldn't be about business. Or don't you remember his shotgun?"

"Oh, I've got that covered. I have the ring. I'll speak with your father, and I'm going to knock your socks off with the most epic proposal."

"Is that so?" She crosses her arms and bites at her lower lip.

My fingers find the juncture of her thighs, but she squeezes her legs together, denying me access. I want to lay her out on the floor, have my way with her, and deal with the future later.

"I'm expecting an unequivocal yes, by the way."

"Is that so?" Her chest rises and falls as her breaths deepen. I put my hands on her knees and force them open. Her legs part with very little resistance. God, I can smell her arousal and that makes my dick ache.

I find it harder and harder to look her in the eyes, especially when I want to bury my head between her legs and lick her until she comes on my face.

"Now what is going on in that head of yours?" she asks.

"I was thinking this is the perfect time to induct you into the mile-high club."

Her attention shifts to the closed door separating us from the cockpit. "And what about him?"

"He won't open that door until we land."

"Is that a regulation?"

"No. I asked him not to."

Her knees slam together. "You did not just tell him we were going to have sex. Dax! Please tell me you didn't."

"I didn't actually." I give a sheepish grin. "I asked him to circle for another hour."

"An hour? You think you'll last that long?"

"Only one way to find out." I put my hands over her knees and pinch until she gives a squeak. Her legs part and I taste victory. But before I kiss her down there...

My mouth crashes down on hers. I kiss her with all of my being, with so much passion that when the intensity of it builds I leave her as breathless as she leaves me.

"I love you, Dani Studer. I think I always have. You're the one I want and I don't want to live without you."

"I love you too, Dax Kingston." She wraps her arms around my neck. "More than I understand if I'm being honest. But I love you." She closes her eyes and the smile on her lips makes my heart skip a beat.

When she opens her eyes, I don't waste anymore time. I lift her off the couch and place her on the floor of the cabin. Maybe I should take more time removing her clothes, but I'm in too much of a rush to slow down.

"I want nothing more than to play out each and every one of my fantasies, but I'm afraid I can't wait. I need to be inside of you."

Her creamy breasts beg for my mouth. In one swift motion, I suck in her nipple, licking and sucking until it tightens into a tiny bud. She moans beneath me, fingers stabbing into my hair as I take my fill. I maneuver out of my pants and shed my briefs. My rigid cock bobs between us, already leaking precum.

I barely remember to sheathe myself. While my cock throbs against her bare stomach, I lavish attention on her nipples making her squirm beneath me. She spreads her legs and I notch my hips between her silken legs. I should wait, tease her a little more, but she takes control away from me when she reaches down and grips my cock. Before I know it, she places the tip against her folds.

"Dax, if you don't put me out of my misery now, I will never say yes."

That is all the encouragement I need. I shift my position and hold her gaze as I slowly push inside. I move an inch, easing in, allowing her to accommodate to my girth. I almost come right there, it feels that good, but I want to do this together.

With every inch I push in, my heart fills with the future this incredible woman promises. This is it, and everything just feels right. She found her way into my heart the moment I caught her broken down by the side of the road.

I move in and out gently, taking my time, delaying my release as she stretches to accept my full length. She wraps her arms around me and digs her heels into my back.

"Don't you dare go slow, or take it easy," she warns. "Fuck me." Her fingernails dig into my ass.

"*Fuuuck!*" I throw my head back.

That's all the permission I need. I lower my head and bite down on her breast as I speed up my pace. She doesn't want slow and gentle, and I won't disappoint. My teeth will leave a mark where I bit her breast, but I want that. I want to mark her in every way.

"*Fuck. Fuck!*" I groan as my mouth moves to the soft skin of her neck, where I lick and suck and bite again, marking her as I go.

I take a fistful of her hair and tug at it while my hips move and moans spill from her mouth. Everything else fades away. There is no engine noise. There is no plane. There is only the sound of our ragged breathing and the slapping of sweat-slicked bodies together as I thrust harder and drive deeper inside of her.

"You're mine," I say with a growl.

That seems to be all it takes, because her body shudders and she calls out my name as her orgasm slams into her. Her muscles pulse around my cock and I can no longer hold off the inevitable. I drive into her faster and deeper as a groan escapes me. My entire body goes rigid with my release. My body ripples with pleasure as we come together.

Kissing her gently, my dick softens inside of her.

"God, but I love you." I leisurely rock my hips, enjoying the gentle aftershocks as I hold her in my arms.

The plane angles down and there's a shift in the whine of the engines. Logan gives us a warning that we'll soon be landing.

I help Dani to her feet and we dress in silence. She keeps giving me secretive glances until I palm her cheeks and lay a kiss on her.

"What are you thinking?"

"That I'm crazy in love with you." She points to Dynamo who's curled up on one of the chairs. He watched us fuck with bland disinterest. "I even love your dog, but it weirds me out when he watches."

"He won't always be watching."

"I hope not, and while we're talking about sex…"

"What?"

She points to her empty ring finger. "We're not having sex again until you put a ring on it."

"Hey, that's not fair!" Not that it matters. "Grandma's ring is in the safe at home. So, I won't have to wait for long. I plan to be back inside of you before dawn breaks." I have no idea what time it is, other than oh-dark-thirty.

Logan flashes the cabin lights and the plane takes a steeper angle down.

"That's our signal." We take our seats and buckle in, all the while Dani keeps an impish grin on her face. "What's so funny?" I glance at her.

"I'm imaging the conversation you'll have with my dad, and wondering if he shoots you with his shotgun for defiling his daughter."

I vent an exasperated sigh. Dynamo looks up and cocks his head.

"For you, I'll face anything because I'm head over heels, crazy in love with you."

I mean every word and will spend the rest of my life showing her exactly how much I love her.

TWENTY-FIVE

Dax

────────

DANI'S LIST OF THREE THINGS RATTLES IN MY HEAD. CONSIDERING her *no sex* declaration until I *put a ring on it,* I find motivation to check things off that list, or convince her to do away with it altogether.

I try. Hell I try really hard.

I take her to my favorite spot at home where we camp out under the stars.

Nope.

She doesn't budge.

Time becomes my enemy and Dani finds wicked pleasure in remaining resolute in her stance to hold out. My arm is getting a workout, easing my ache, not that jerking off satisfies my hunger. When I have the chance, I vow to make her pay for my suffering.

Dani's Spring Break comes to an end, which means it's time to take her home.

I consult with my father over the phone, tracking my father's recovery, and set up a deal I hope Tom Studer can't turn down.

When Dani and I arrive at Crowbar Ranch, I meet the business end of a shotgun. Dynamo jumps out of the truck, happy to be home, or what the dog considers home and trots up to Studer. Tongue lolling. Tail wagging. Dynamo greets Studer with the carefree abandon only a dog can manage.

Studer reaches down to scratch between Dynamo's ears, but doesn't lower the shotgun aimed at my chest.

"Daddy!" Dani's flustered screech does nothing to assuage her father. "Put that thing down."

"You get inside." Studer waves to the open front door. "And get away from him."

Dani tosses an apologetic look over her shoulder and mouths *Good luck! You'll need it.* Then she glides across the dusty ground and heads inside, leaving me and her father facing each other down.

I have the ring. One box checked. Now to get her father's blessing.

It takes grit and a lot of balls to return and face Studer. I do that with a sureness inside of me that I'll die a thousand deaths before I give up Dani's hand in marriage.

Studer and I will work out our differences across the barrel of his shotgun if we have to, but we will work shit out.

"Sir, I can explain."

"You'd better explain where you took my daughter. Three days and no word? I've a mind to shoot you where you stand for kidnapping her like that."

"I can assure you, there was no kidnapping involved."

"I call it like I see it." He glances inside, checking on his daughter, never once letting the barrel of his gun waver.

"Actually, I have something I'd like to discuss."

"We're not discussing anything." He gestures with his gun. "You get back in that truck and don't think about coming back."

"You haven't heard what I have to say."

"Don't care what you have to say."

I shrug. "That deal you struck with Scott's family is a shit deal. Are you aware they're going to rob you blind?"

The widening of Studer's eyes says I score a direct hit. Studer may have suspected, but he has no idea of the extent of the thievery. I press the advantage, not giving Studer time to regroup.

"You're sitting on millions and they kept it from you. The measly payout they're offering is a fraction of what your land is worth. I have an alternate proposition, one that solves your problems and ensures Crowbar Ranch stays in your family."

Studer's eyes narrow. "You seem to be talking big for a drifter."

"What do you know about Kingston Ranch and its affiliates?"

A wise businessman, if Studer knows anything about ranching, he knows Kingston Industries. The barrel of his gun dips and he cocks his head, likely putting the pieces together.

"What do *you* know about them?" He turns the question around, giving me the perfect opening.

"We're willing to offer a limited partnership."

"We?"

"Me and my father, Seth Kingston."

Studer puts the safety on his shotgun and lowers the weapon. "You Seth Kingston's boy? You're one of those Kingstons?"

I never hid my name from Studer. It's not my fault Studer never connected the dots, not that I made it easy.

"I am."

"And you're just now telling me this?" The look that passes across Studer's face is one of shock and disbelief.

"I have a vested interest in getting back into your good graces."

"And why is that?"

I don't know if Dani watches through the windows, but my intent is no secret.

"I plan on marrying your daughter, and I need your blessing before I bend a knee." That's step three.

Studer will not deny me my future.

"Is that so?" Studer leans the shotgun against the wall.

"If I have your blessing, of course."

"Well, there may not be any land to annex into Kingston Industries. Loans are due tomorrow. The ranch is pretty much gone."

"That's not a problem."

"It's not a small bit of cash."

"Not a problem. One call and it's done, but I'd like to discuss the terms with you first. You need to know what you have on the table, the things Scott's family kept from you."

"Does it matter?" Studer's eyes narrow. "One way or the other, I'm losing my land. To him. Or to you."

No way in hell is Scott's silly offer still on the table.

"See, that's where you're wrong. You retain full control. All assets remain within the Studer family and right of survivorship passes only to direct decedents." I'll marry Dani, but her land stays in her family.

"You don't want my land?"

"I have plenty in Texas, but I can show you how to turn things around."

"And these mineral rights you found?"

"Frankly you don't need them if you change a few of the things you're currently doing. My father is big on conservation. Not that you can't tap some of those mineral reserves, but if you do, we'll show you how to do it with the least impact to the land."

Studer glances over his shoulder and scratches his chin. "I'm thinking this involves a longer conversation."

"How about we take this to Marge's Diner? We can discuss everything." I sweep an arm toward the passenger door of my truck. I'll have Studer's blessing by the end of the day. Dani has to leave tonight to make it back to the first day of classes after Spring Break and there's no way I'm leaving without taking her to bed again.

The next few months will be a long, lonely separation while she finishes out her third year and I take over operations back in Texas.

"All right. You have my ear."

"Great, I'll just get Dani."

Studer shakes his head. "Dani stays. This conversation doesn't involve her."

"I disagree."

Studer glances down at the shotgun and dusts off the rim of the barrel. He cocks an eyebrow and gives me a hard stare. "Son, this conversation happens without her. You hear me?"

"Yes, sir."

Dani's father turns around and enters the house, leaving the door wide open as he disappears inside. Traitorous Dynamo follows the rancher in, making himself right at home. There's some yelling, and I head for the door. Studer meets me back on the porch with a light jacket tossed over his shoulder and a scowl fixed on his face.

"You coming?" He marches to the truck and climbs into the passenger seat.

I peek inside and catch Dani standing in the living room, hands on her hips and head shaking with disbelief.

"You okay?" I call out.

She lifts a finger and makes a spinning gesture. "You'd better go with him and good luck."

She might have her list of three things, but Dani wants this as much as I do. There isn't the smallest bit of doubt in my mind, but the expression on her face is troubled. I take a step inside, but she shakes her head.

"Seriously, Dax, don't keep him waiting."

"I want to hold you in my arms."

She points behind me. "I'm fine. My dad though? I'm not so sure he's okay with this thing between us."

Suppressing a growl, my fingers clench. "I'll be back for you."

TWENTY-SIX

Epilogue

"DANI!" I CALL UP THE STAIRS. "WE'RE GOING TO BE LATE."

My time in the Air Force hammered punctuality into my genetic makeup. On-time is late. Early is on time.

And we're going to be very, very late.

I don't want to go to this thing, but it's a rare day Dani gets to reconnect with her friends from high school. She also wants to show off her engagement ring.

Dani Studer will become Dani Kingston.

Well, after she graduates from veterinary school, and after her veterinary practice is set up. Those are the conditions her father placed before giving his blessing. Our engagement will be much longer than I want, but I'm content to wait.

I have the girl.

I'll work with my father to groom a successor to manage the Kingston lands in Texas. I'll oversee the entirety of Kingston Industries from Bear Creek, an unlikely home, but exactly where I want to be. Her father didn't ask for that, but it means a lot to him to keep his daughter close. I'm happy to honor that wish.

"Dani!" What the hell is she doing? It's a simple barbecue.

"I'm coming!"

Ten minutes later, I shut the door on my truck. Dynamo settles into the back seat and takes up position with his nose plastered to the window. Without a word, I grit my teeth and head down the long drive toward Caleb and Cate's ranch.

It's going to be a reunion, and according to Dani, the first time the gang has been together since high school. Brent, Caleb, and Erika took time off to pursue their dreams right after graduation.

Brent uncovered sunken treasure and then lost some of it to modern-day pirates, while Caleb went on to become a Delta operative. He and Cate are high school sweethearts who managed to find each other after a separation which seemed far too long.

I'm the new guy on the block, but Dani says it doesn't matter. Brent brings his fiancée, Brie. Somehow that makes everything all right.

The big news and the reason for the get-together is Commander Erika Black. The Coast Guard cutter captain is home on leave.

"I'm so excited." Dani bounces in the passenger seat. "Cate just called. Erika's plane is a little delayed."

I believe that. Montana weather can be notoriously unpredictable.

"I love your enthusiasm." I reach over and squeeze her thigh.

"You love everything about me." She speaks with absolute assurance, and why wouldn't she? Dani is one-hundred percent right.

"Truth." I grip the wheel. "I'd love to pull over and fuck you on the side of the road. What do you think about a little truck sex before meeting your friends?"

"Eww."

"Eww? Why eww? Way to kill a guy's ego." I place my hand over my chest as if wounded.

"It's not you. Dynamo always stares at me, and I'm not meeting my friends with freshly fucked hair. It took me forever to get it to look like this."

Did she do something special?

"You look great."

"Thanks."

I love everything about my bride-to-be and can't wait to put a ring on her finger for good.

"You know, we could just turn around and spend a night at home...alone."

It's been months since we've had the house to ourselves. Once her father gave his blessing, I moved into the main house, but not into Dani's bed. Her father insists on separate bedrooms until we're actually wed.

However, her father is currently in Texas, meeting with my father about plans for streamlining the operations of his ranch. Which means, I'm missing a golden opportunity to have Dani all to myself for the night.

Dani gives me the run down, one more time, on her friends. I know all about Caleb and Cate. Caleb and I bonded over the injuries which cut our military careers short. Brent recovered billions in Spanish gold somewhere off the Florida Keys, then promptly had some of it stolen by pirates. I know nothing about Erika, except out of the entire crew, she seems to be the only one not married, engaged, or otherwise attached.

We pull up and park outside Caleb and Cate's home. Before I can put the truck in park, Dani jumps out of the truck and squeals at the top of her lungs. She and Cate hug. Another woman exits the house and joins the happy friends. She reaches out and takes Brent's hand.

"Come on, Dynamo. The party is starting."

Dynamo hops out of the truck and greets everyone with the enthusiasm only a dog can muster. I follow behind and take the first opportunity to pull Dani to my side. She squeals as I steal a kiss.

"Dax," she says, "this is Brent and his fiancée Brie."

I shove out my hand and shake with Brent, then give Brie a kiss on the cheek. "Nice to meet you."

"Likewise," Brent says.

Brent, Cate, and Dani head inside which leaves me and Brie out on the lawn with Dynamo.

"Are you as terrified as me?" she asks.

"We're the outsiders." I give her a slow nod and a wink.

"Soon to be outlaws," she teases. "I heard you and Dani are engaged?"

"We are, although her father is dead set on waiting until Dani is done with all her schooling."

"I can understand that." Brie lowers her voice to a whisper. "As the outsiders, we need to stick together."

"I prefer outlaws. But, I agree we need to stick together. Nice to meet you."

She takes my hand and we exaggerate the shake like we're in cahoots with each other. "Likewise." Brie's kind of cool. I like her immediately.

"Well, shall we join the festivities?"

"If we must." Brie glances toward the house and gives a dramatic sigh.

"I hear you're a boat captain."

We drift off into casual conversation about our careers and how we met our soon to be spouses.

After we join the others, beer and wine flows with the same rapidity as the conversation. I join Caleb out back with Brent to monitor the progress of the *roast beast*. At least that's what Caleb calls it.

While the girls catch up inside, we tend the grill and exchange tall tales. Brent turns out to be a really cool guy. He tells us how he met Brie and about the treasure he recovered.

"So what happens next?" I ask. "Is all the treasure gone?"

"Well," Brent says, "they only got a little bit of it. It took a few weeks for us to pull the rest of it up, but they did get away with some priceless artifacts."

"And you get to keep it all?"

"Oh no. The treasure belongs to the Spanish government, but there's a finder's fee."

"Really?" I have a feeling that finder's fee is no small thing.

Brent doesn't elaborate and I don't push. I grew up with wealth and it's bad manners to pry.

A short while later, Cate pokes her head out the back door. "Brent, Erika is five-minutes out."

Everyone's been waiting for Erika to arrive. Brent and Caleb aren't the only ones who left Bear Creek and rarely make it back.

Like them, this is the first time in years that Erika's come home. But I understand the pull. She's making a name for herself in the Coast Guard. There are very few females with her rank and billet as captain to one of the ultra-elite cutters.

Brent jogs inside at the news.

"Do you mind tending the beast?" Caleb asks.

"Absolutely." As Caleb clearly wants to greet Erika with all his friends, I take over responsibility for the grill. While everyone waits inside for Erika's arrival, I turn to the grill and consider how lucky I am to have stumbled upon a dog who led me to Bear Creek.

A short time later, everyone tumbles out the back door and spills onto the lawn. I'm introduced to Erika while Caleb brings me a fresh beer. It's time to take the *roast beast* off the grill to rest and I carry it inside while the others stack wood in the fire pit.

We sit around a campfire and chat about everything and nothing, a group of friends spending a night together as if the years separating them never happened.

Dani sits in my lap, and for the first time in a very long time, I feel like I've found home.

"Oh!" Erika says to Brent. "I didn't tell you, but we have a lead."

"What?" Brent's shout draws everyone's attention and silences all conversation. "You're kidding?"

"Nope." Erika shakes her head. "Give me a few months and I bet we recover that stolen Spanish gold."

Everybody lifts their bottles in a toast to take down the evil pirates.

As for myself, I tug Dani to my side and whisper in her ear.

"You're the one I want. You know that?"

She cups my chin and presses her lips to my temple.

"Yes, and you know what I want to do tonight?"

My brows lift and I try to think of a snarky response, but she leans close and whispers in my ear.

"I want to camp by the river. You know where I mean?"

How can I forget?

"And I want to watch you walk out of the river buck naked and save me with your rope."

"I can think of nothing more I'd rather do." I hold her tight and work to hide my raging erection.

There's still dinner to get through, and more sitting around the campfire trading tall tales. I'm going to have blue balls before the evening is through.

But I don't care. I have the best girl in the world, a future filled with endless possibilities, and a heart that's overflowing. I stare at Dani and smile.

I can't believe I found the one woman I can't live without, and I'm eager to continue our life together.

THANK YOU FOR READING DAX AND DANI'S STORY. WE HOPE YOU enjoyed spending some time beneath the Montana sun.

Be sure to check out Saving Jen. See what happens when a city erupts in violence and a couple finds their second chance at love.

Get your copy of Saving Jen today. Click HERE.

A story of the deepest love, tragic loss, and a chance for *Redemption*.

Jennifer:

While our cities burn, I face devastation on the streets, saving lives while my marriage falls apart. I once thought Patton and I could survive anything, but we're not coming out of this unscathed. We've lost too much and our love is stretched beyond the breaking point. The choices I make aren't easy, but at the end of a long and brutal night, I'll see what remains of both my city and the love of the man I can't live without.

Patton:

Overcome with grief, I walked away. The love of my life is on the streets, doing what she does best. Jen's saving lives, but when she goes missing in the middle of the riots, I can no longer ignore the truth. She's my wife. My love. She's my life. I may not be worthy of redemption, but I will bring my wife home.

Will the riots and civil unrest destroy Patton and Jennifer's second chance for a happily ever after? Or does fate have something else in store?

Saving Jen is **a steamy, second chance, contemporary romantic suspense. It features a protective hero and the smart, feisty heroine who steals his heart.**

(Saving Jen was previously published as Patton.)

If you're enjoying The One I Want series and love contemporary romance we think you'll love reading Heart's Insanity, book 1 in the Angel Fire Rock Romance series.

Skye Summers endured a tragic past. She wants what the past stole, and despite lingering scars, she's surviving and thriving. Now she cures the sick, heals the wounded, and takes care of those clinging to life. The only person she can't heal is herself, because Skye is too broken for love.

Ash Dean has it all: Fame, fortune, and the adoration of screaming fans. The constant parties, drugs, alcohol, and an endless string of one-night stands are taking their toll. He gives and his fans take, until he's lost within the crowd. He wants someone to see him for the man he wishes to be rather than the one he's become.

One fate…

Two lives…

Three Days…

That's the proposition…

It would be insane to accept and Skye's a fool to agree, but she's tired of playing it safe.

It's time to take a leap of faith, besides what could go wrong?

You can grab Ash & Skye's story.

Just click HERE.

And of course, if you enjoyed Dax & Dani's story, we'd love to hear what you thought. Please consider leaving a review. A sentence is all it takes and we certainly appreciate every word!

THANK YOU FOR READING DAX & DANI'S STORY. WE HOPE YOU enjoyed spending some time beneath the Montana sun.

If you enjoyed The One I Want series and love contemporary romance we think you'll love reading Heart's Insanity, book 1 in the Angel Fire Rock Romance series.

SKYE SUMMERS ENDURED A TRAGIC PAST. SHE WANTS WHAT THE PAST stole, and despite lingering scars, she's surviving and thriving. Now she cures the sick, heals the wounded, and takes care of those clinging to life. The only person she can't heal is herself, because Skye is too broken for love.

Ash Dean has it all: Fame, fortune, and the adoration of screaming fans. The constant parties, drugs, alcohol, and an endless string of one-night stands are taking their toll. He gives and his fans take, until he's lost within the crowd. He wants someone to see him for the man he wishes to be rather than the one he's become.

One fate…

Two lives…

Three Days…

That's the proposition…

It would be insane to accept and Skye's a fool to agree, but she's tired of playing it safe.

It's time to take a leap of faith, besides what could go wrong?

You can grab Ash & Skye's story.

Just click HERE.

And of course, if you enjoyed Dax & Dani's story, we'd love to hear what you thought. Please consider leaving a review. A sentence is all it takes and we certainly appreciate every word!

TWENTY-SEVEN

Sneak Peak at Saving Jen

THE RADIO ON JENNIFER GALLOWAY'S HIP SQUAWKED TO LIFE. *SHOTS fired. Multiple injuries.*

This doesn't sound good. She braced herself for a rough scene.

Dispatch gave the location; a park about fifteen blocks away.

Erik Langley, senior paramedic, her mentor, and her husband's best friend, cursed and threw down a twenty while she grabbed the bag containing their sandwiches. Bag and drinks in hand, she followed Erik out of the sandwich shop, dodging the people walking in.

Erik was tall like her husband, although not as muscular, but like Patton he had a presence about him. People jumped out of Erik's way, and she followed in his wake, gripping the sandwiches they would never have time to eat.

Once outside, he yanked on the door of their rig, jumped in, and latched his seatbelt. He cranked the ignition and flipped on lights and sirens to herald their way through the congested city.

The call continued, filling in pertinent details. She scribbled notes while Erik took a long swallow of soda. The call wasn't that far from where they had stopped for a quick bite, but it would take them into an area known for gang turf wars.

Her husband would be pissed. Patton had been after her for over a year to transfer out of the San Francisco area and take a position at NorthBay Regional Medical Center, closer to home; especially now that she was pregnant again.

She'd lost their first two pregnancies. He said nothing outright, but he blamed the rigors of her job for the miscarriages. This was the longest she had carried a pregnancy, and so far, things looked good. Eighteen weeks didn't seem like a long time, but for her, every day came as a blessing. Not out of the woods yet, she allowed herself to hope. They needed this child, but anything which took her into danger brought out Patton's protectiveness.

To keep him happy, she had put in a request to transfer from San Francisco to Fairfield. Erik had as well. Although NorthBay paid less than San Francisco, he was willing to take the pay cut instead of losing his partner.

They pulled up to the intersection. People gawked and blocked the sidewalk, facing in toward a small neighborhood park. No one was helping the victims. That had become an all too common occurrence and had her questioning human nature.

"We're the first to arrive." She braced for the nasty job of triage.

"The other crews should be here soon."

She jumped out, stethoscope flapping around her neck, and slung a small medical kit over her shoulder. Erik would head to the rear, pull out the stretcher, and meet her with a larger bag of medical supplies.

Those gathered parted only after some prodding. It amazed her how the mind of the crowd worked. They weren't helping the wounded, yet prevented her from getting to them, giving nasty looks like she had no right to shove. Did they think she pushed through to get a better view?

"Excuse me," she called out, elbowing her way between the bystanders.

The cries of a woman sliced through the air. Another man groaned. When she forced her way through the final ranks of those gathered, the scene came into crystal clear focus. A patch of green at the corner of the street had been turned into a small community park. A tiny kids' area had a rickety metal slide and a rusty swing set. Two metal picnic tables filled the rest of the space, and patchy turf struggled to survive underfoot.

The blaring of another siren sounded on the streets. Good. Other teams would be there soon.

A groaning man clutched at his thigh. Blood stained his pants and oozed between his fingers. Beside him, another man propped himself against the slide. He gripped his shoulder and winced with pain. She continued her scan, taking a few seconds to tally the injuries and decide who needed her most. A woman hunched over the picnic bench. Blood stained her shirt. She'd been shot in the gut. A crying woman sat by the swing set and held the lifeless body of a little girl in her arms.

Jen raced to the mother. A bullet grazed her upper arm. The little girl stared up into the sky. No signs of life. Jen felt for a pulse, knowing she wouldn't find one, then placed a hand on the grieving woman's shoulder. Was she the mother? No time to ask.

"I'm so very sorry."

"Holly! My little girl. She's gone." Tears rushed down the woman's face, and she clutched the little girl tight to her breast, swaying in terrible anguish.

Sirens blared. More help was on the way.

Jen headed to the woman by the picnic table who looked to have the most life-threatening injury. The two men could wait. Erik made his way through the crowd and she pointed to each victim, calling out the injuries.

"Abdominal wound here. Leg. Shoulder."

"Gotcha." He lowered the stretcher to the ground and opened the bag of supplies.

"Ma'am, my name is Jen and I will take care of you. What's your name?"

"Juanita." The woman huffed against the pain.

Jen raised the woman's blouse and inspected the damage. Entry with an exit wound. That was helpful. It was worse when bullets stayed inside the body; they shredded internal organs and vessels. That kind of damage wasn't easily assessed on site. Fashioning a field bandage, she packed a pressure dressing around the woman's wound.

Erik went to evaluate the two men and came back only after other ambulance crews showed up. By then, she had an IV placed and her first set of vitals recorded.

"Need help?"

"Breathing's fine. I started an IV. Help me get her on the stretcher."

They worked together to get the woman secured. Extending the stretcher to its full height, Erik took off toward their rig while she checked in with the other crews. They had their victims well in hand. With a final glance over her shoulder, Jen couldn't help but linger on the poor woman holding a dead child in her arms.

As she walked back to the rig, snippets of conversation drifted to her ears.

"This is why we need more cops on the streets." An elderly man's frustrated shout cut through those gathered.

"More cops don't do no good, Jerome, not when they're paid to stay off our streets."

"That ain't true."

"You think it ain't? I tell you, them there cops are paid to go away."

Erik held open the back doors of their rig and Jen jumped in. The voices of those in the crowd turned angry, accusations about police turning a blind eye and taking bribes to disappear floated in the air. It was time to leave before things got any more heated.

The doors shut with a solid *thunk* and Erik slapped the door from the outside. Moving around to the driver's side, he hopped in. "You all set?"

She double checked the bar securing the stretcher and gave Erik a thumbs up. "Ready."

He called in to dispatch. "Female, 35, bullet to abdomen, exit wound present. Conscious, alert, vitals: heart rate 115, respirations non-labored, radial pulse strong. Normal Saline running. Trauma Team required. ETA ten minutes."

He took the streets fast, siren blaring, and Jen held on tight in the back. Her patient was conscious and responding to questions. Jen took down as much information as possible and checked the bandage for excessive bleeding. Despite the gunshot, the woman was doing remarkably well.

When they parked outside the emergency department, Jen gathered her things. Erik popped open the back doors, released the stabilizing bar, and pulled the stretcher out until the wheels hit the ground.

She followed behind, reassuring their patient. Although summer, the Bay Area temperatures remained cool, hovering in the low seventies. Despite that, perspiration pooled under her armpits and the crotch of her pants felt tacky and wet.

"Jen," Erik called, his voice concerned. "Is that the patient's blood?"

She glanced at the dark stain between her legs.

"No! No! No!" Collapsing back on the side bench, she clutched at her belly. *Not again.*

Erik called for extra help, surprising the emergency department staff with not one but two patients.

"You didn't tell me you were pregnant." His tone was both chastising and concerned. "How far along are you?"

"Eighteen weeks."

She couldn't afford to lose another baby, not with the growing rift between her and Patton. He wanted this child as much, or more than she and he had decorated the spare bedroom in their house. So far, he'd only painted the walls, but he'd purchased one of those sliding recliners for breastfeeding and the search history on their shared computer showed him checking out cribs and wall decor, girl, boy, and gender neutral. They didn't know the sex and still debated if they wanted to.

A nurse came to the back of the ambulance, pushing a wheelchair. "What's wrong with her?"

"Miscarriage." Erik glanced at Jen's crotch and his lips tightened. "Doesn't that seem like a lot of blood?"

"We've got her," the nurse said. "Ma'am, can I help you down?"

Erik and the nurse helped Jen into the wheelchair and she settled in. With as much blood as she lost, shouldn't it hurt? She felt nothing.

No cramping.

No pain.

Nothing.

She hadn't even realized she'd been bleeding, thinking the wetness had been nervous perspiration.

Erik gripped her hand and gave a reassuring squeeze. "I'll call Patton and let him know."

She returned a tight nod. How would her husband receive this news? Would he hate her for failing to protect their unborn child? All she wanted was to curl in on herself and cry.

SEE WHAT HAPPENS WHEN A CITY ERUPTS IN VIOLENCE AND A COUPLE finds their second chance at love.

Get your copy of Saving Jen today. Click HERE.

ELLZ BELLZ

ELLIE'S FACEBOOK READER GROUP

If you are interested in joining the ELLZ BELLZ, Ellie's Facebook reader group, we'd love to have you.

Join Ellie's ELLZ BELLZ.
The ELLZ BELLZ Facebook Reader Group

Sign up for Ellie's Newsletter.
Elliemasters.com/newslettersignup

Also by Ellie Masters

The LIGHTER SIDE

Ellie Masters is the lighter side of the Jet & Ellie Masters writing duo! You will find Contemporary Romance, Military Romance, Romantic Suspense, Billionaire Romance, and Rock Star Romance in Ellie's Works.

YOU CAN FIND ELLIE'S BOOKS HERE:

ELLIEMASTERS.COM/BOOKS

Military Romance

Guardian Hostage Rescue Specialists

Rescuing Melissa

(Get a FREE copy of Rescuing Melissa

when you join Ellie's Newsletter

https://elliemasters.com/RescuingMelissa)

Rescuing Zoe

Rescuing Moira

Rescuing Eve

Rescuing Lily

Rescuing Jinx

Rescuing Maria

Military Romance

Guardian Personal Protection Specialists

Sybil's Protector

The One I Want Series

(Small Town, Military Heroes)

By Jet & Ellie Masters

EACH BOOK IN THIS SERIES CAN BE READ AS A STANDALONE AND IS ABOUT A DIFFERENT COUPLE WITH AN HEA.

Saving Ariel

Saving Brie

Saving Cate

Saving Dani

Saving Jen

Saving Abby

Rockstar Romance

The Angel Fire Rock Romance Series

EACH BOOK IN THIS SERIES CAN BE READ AS A STANDALONE AND IS ABOUT A DIFFERENT COUPLE WITH AN HEA. IT IS RECOMMENDED THEY ARE READ IN ORDER.

Ashes to New (prequel)

Heart's Insanity (book 1)

Heart's Desire (book 2)

Heart's Collide (book 3)

Hearts Divided (book 4)

Hearts Entwined (book5)

Forest's FALL (book 6)

Hearts The Last Beat (book7)

Contemporary Romance

Firestorm

(KRISTY BROMBERG'S EVERYDAY HEROES WORLD)

Billionaire Romance

Billionaire Boys Club

Hawke

Richard

Brody

Contemporary Romance

Cocky Captain

(Vi Keeland & Penelope Ward's Cocky Hero World)

Romantic Suspense

EACH BOOK IS A STANDALONE NOVEL.

The Starling

~AND~

Science Fiction

Ellie Masters writing as L.A. Warren

Vendel Rising: a Science Fiction Serialized Novel

About the Author

ELLIE MASTERS is a multi-genre and Amazon Top 100 best-selling author, writing the stories she loves to read. These are dark erotic tales. Or maybe, sweet contemporary stories. How about a romantic thriller to whet your appetite? Ellie writes it all. Want to read passionate poems and sensual secrets? She does that, too. Dip into the eclectic mind of Ellie Masters, spend time exploring the sensual realm where she breathes life into her characters and brings them from her mind to the page and into the heart of her readers every day.

Ellie Masters has been exploring the worlds of romance, dark erotica, science fiction, and fantasy by writing the stories she wants to read. When not writing, Ellie can be found outside, where her passion for all things outdoor reigns supreme: off-roading, riding ATVs, scuba diving, hiking, and breathing fresh air are top on her list.

She has lived all over the United States—east, west, north, south and central—but grew up under the Hawaiian sun. She's also been privileged to have lived overseas, experiencing other cultures and making lifelong friends. Now, Ellie is proud to call herself a Southern transplant, learning to say y'all and "bless her heart" with the best of them. She lives with her beloved husband, two children who refuse to flee the nest, and four fur-babies; three cats who rule the household, and a dog who wants nothing other than for the cats to be his best friends. The cats have a different opinion regarding this matter.

Ellie's favorite way to spend an evening is curled up on a couch, laptop in place, watching a fire, drinking a good wine, and bringing forth all the characters from her mind to the page and hopefully into the hearts of her readers.

FOR MORE INFORMATION
elliemasters.com

facebook.com/elliemastersromance

twitter.com/Ellie__Masters

instagram.com/ellie_masters

bookbub.com/authors/ellie-masters

goodreads.com/Ellie_Masters

Connect with Ellie Masters

Website:
elliemasters.com
Amazon Author Page:
elliemasters.com/amazon
Facebook:
elliemasters.com/Facebook
Goodreads:
elliemasters.com/Goodreads
Instagram:
elliemasters.com/Instagram

Final Thoughts

I hope you enjoyed this book as much as I enjoyed writing it. If you enjoyed reading this story, please consider leaving a review on Amazon and Goodreads, and please let other people know. A sentence is all it takes. Friend recommendations are the strongest catalyst for readers' purchase decisions! And I'd love to be able to continue bringing the characters and stories from My-Mind-to-the-Page.

Second, call or e-mail a friend and tell them about this book. If you really want them to read it, gift it to them. If you prefer digital friends, please use the "Recommend" feature of Goodreads to spread the word.

Or visit my blog https://elliemasters.com, where you can find out more about my writing process and personal life.

Come visit The EDGE: Dark Discussions where we'll have a chance to talk about my works, their creation, and maybe what the future has in store for my writing.

Facebook Reader Group: Ellz Bellz

Thank you so much for your support!

Love,

Ellie

Dedication

This book is dedicated to you, my reader. Thank you for spending a few hours of your time with me. I wouldn't be able to write without you to cheer me on. Your wonderful words, your support, and your willingness to join me on this journey is a gift beyond measure.

Whether this is the first book of mine you've read, or if you've been with me since the very beginning, thank you for believing in me as I bring these characters 'from my mind to the page and into your hearts.'

Love,

Ellie

THE END